W9-DEU-985

Return to:

Pacific Northwest
Children's Literature Clearinghouse
MH 254
School of Education
Western Washington University
Bellingham, WA 98225

THROUGH THE
OPEN DOOR

THROUGH THE OPEN DOOR

Joy N. Hulme

HarperCollins*Publishers*

Library of Congress Cataloging-in-Publication Data
Hulme, Joy N.
  Through the open door / Joy N. Hulme.
    p.   cm.
  Rev. ed. of: The other side of the door. c1990.
  Summary: Nine-year-old Dora, who has been kept out of school because of
her speech impediment, dreams of learning to speak normally as her family
joins a group of other Mormons journeying from Utah to New Mexico in
1910.
  ISBN 0-380-97870-9
  [1. Speech disorders—Fiction.   2. Frontier and pioneer life—Fiction.
3. New Mexico—Fiction.   4. Mormons—Fiction.]   I. Hulme, Joy N.
Other side of the door.   II. Title.
PZ7.H8845 Th   2000   00-21651
[Fic]—dc21   CIP
                                                                    AC

1   2   3   4   5   6   7   8   9   10
❖
First Edition

PREVIOUSLY PUBLISHED IN DIFFERENT FORM AS *THE OTHER SIDE OF THE DOOR*
BY DESERET BOOK COMPANY, 1991.

Author's Note

Through the Open Door and other books to follow are based on true incidents in the life of a real person. I visited with the original Dora* on a regular basis while she lived her final days in a rest home. My motive was to cheer her up. Instead, she was the one who kept the encounters lively, with colorful reminiscences about her childhood, spent growing up in a large family on a homestead farm in New Mexico. Without any money to spare, the Cooksons were forced to use their ingenuity to solve their problems. Visit after visit, I left the rest home saying, "Someone should write a book about that." Finally, it became clear that *I* was the logical person to make a written record about this creative family.

In the months that followed, Dora and I established a regular routine as I collected her stories. I wrote one incident each week and read it to her while we enjoyed a picnic in the park at lunchtime. Occasionally, when some small detail was missing, I'd fill in from my own experience or imagination. She always noticed and said, "How did you know that? I didn't tell you, but you got it just right." The reason I knew was that we were kindred spirits.

After we reviewed each adventure, she'd share another. My friend had an incredible memory, a playful sense of humor, and a picturesque way of speaking. She was delighted that an account of

---

* The names of all the characters have been changed.

so many parts of her life was being written down. I was having fun doing it.

By the time Dora died in 1975, I had collected about thirty-five incidents. I had a lot to learn about putting them into a book, however. It took years and years of trial and error and considerable study. During that time, my husband and I recreated the covered wagon journey from Salt Lake City to Clovis, New Mexico, to become acquainted with the terrain and towns along the way and to verify the details of Dora's story. Everything we could check on proved to be true. We visited with people who knew the family and even found some members who still lived there. We were led to the real, tumbling down, homestead house and found the recorded deed to the property in the county courthouse. I studied the history of New Mexico and perused microfilms of the newspapers printed during the ten years covered by Dora's story. My own experiences and imagination contributed as well. The writing of this book has been a long journey. Dora did grow from the conversations of two kindred spirits, but in the end she came to life as her own self, and *Through the Open Door* is her story.

THROUGH THE OPEN DOOR

CHAPTER ONE

HEARING THE NEWS

It's awful to be the first one to know the good news and not be able to tell it. No matter how much I wanted to spread the exciting message, a girl who can't talk can't tell.

When I heard Papa explaining to Mama what was going to happen to our family in the fall of 1910, I wanted to let Caroline, Ed, and everyone else know about it. But I couldn't. No matter how hard I tried, I'd never been able to make words come out of my mouth so they could be understood. Every time I opened my lips to speak, the sounds were all mixed up and mushy—more like grunts and groans than speaking.

Because I couldn't talk, I was considered stupid—too stupid to learn. I wasn't allowed to go to school, so I'd never been taught to read or write.

I could usually get what I wanted by nudging the person next to me and pointing to whatever I needed. I used hand movements or facial expressions to make my meaning clear. I drew pictures. I could say *yes* or *no* with a nod or shake of my head, but explaining anything was almost impossible. Some words just have to be spoken or the message gets all mixed up. Trying to get my ideas to come out the right way made me feel like a corked-up bottle with yeast growing inside—swollen and tight, ready to explode.

Members of my family were used to the way I was. Mama and Papa loved me deeply and encouraged me to develop other talents. They seemed to take it for granted that my speechless condition was hopeless. Caroline sometimes tried to pretend she didn't know me in front of her friends. Ed was my best pal. He worked hardest to understand me. Other children either ignored or teased me; adults acted as if I were not there at all. I hated it when a group of gossipy ladies huddled together in a circle at church to feel sorry for me, even when I was close enough to hear what they said. They acted as if I couldn't hear any better than I could speak.

"Isn't it too bad about that pretty little Cookson girl?"

"She can't say a word so you can understand it."

"Sounds like she's got a mouthful of hot mush."

"No wonder they won't let her go to school. What would a poor teacher do?"

I wanted to shout, "A poor teacher would let me listen! *There's nothing wrong with my brain!*"

It seemed to me that any teacher would be glad to have me. I'd be the quietest nine-year-old in the room. I'd already proved I wasn't any trouble in a Sunday School class.

I should have been entering fourth grade. Caroline was in fifth, Ed was in third, and I was like the middle of a sandwich between them. Even six-year-old Frank had started school and was learning to read.

I hated staying home, especially in the afternoon, when my youngest brothers, George and Howie, took their naps. I always had to figure out something quiet to do while they were asleep. That's why I was playing house under the trailing branches of the weeping willow tree that sunny September day, when I heard Papa talking to Mama on the back porch. While she folded the clean clothes she'd just taken off the line, he told her what was about to happen.

He was excited! Even though he started in a whisper so he wouldn't wake the little boys, his words soon came out louder and louder and faster and faster. I tied my twin handkerchief dolls to a branch, where a breeze would rock them to sleep, and moved quietly to the bottom step to listen.

"Oh, hon," Papa exclaimed, "our prayers are going to be answered at last!"

"How's that?" Mama asked.

"A golden opportunity is knocking at the door," Papa told her. "We're finally going to have a place of our own. Just imagine what it will be like to own a whole farm!"

Papa paused, as if he were considering that idea. I could just imagine the smile on his face.

After a minute or two, he went on. "We've known for a long time that Dad's twenty acres here in Utah can't stretch far enough to divide between all of his children. Sooner or later some of us will have to leave. Well, now's our chance. This is the time."

"And just where is this Garden of Eden that you have in mind?" Mama asked.

"New Mexico," Papa said. "Clovis, New Mexico. There's some homesteading opportunities down there."

"You mean some of that land the government gives away to new settlers?"

"They don't exactly *give* it away," Papa said. "We'd have to *earn* it."

"How?" Mama asked.

"By living on it and raising crops," Papa told her.

"I thought homesteading days were over," Mama said. "Isn't all that free land used up?"

"Most of it," Papa agreed. "But some of the Clovis settlers decided not to stay on their farms. They gave up their claims. Now the government owns those pieces again, so they are available for other families."

"How come this golden opportunity happened to knock on *our* door?" Mama wanted to know.

"Clem Coldwell got a letter from his brother-in-law, who's in charge of the government land office in New Mexico," Papa told her. "John Talbot's his name. He has twelve homesteads to assign and has offered to save them for Clem and his Utah friends. Clem asked me if we'd like to go."

"That's nice of him," Mama said. After a pause, she asked, "How much land is there in a homestead farm?"

"A hundred and sixty acres," Papa told her. "That's eight times as big as Dad's place. Just imagine all that room to grow anything we want—corn, beans, potatoes, and . . ." he raised his voice to make sure I heard . . . *"plenty of watermelons for dear little Dora . . ."*

I imagined a whole field of my favorite fruit. Rows and rows of fat green melons all ready to cut into smile-shaped wedges. My mouth began to water at the very thought.

Every year Papa bought us a big watermelon to celebrate the Fourth of July. Mama led us all outside before she cut the round slices and divided them in halves.

"We'll let the juice spill on the grass," she said, "so the floor doesn't get sticky."

We gobbled up the crisp, red centers and had contests to see how far we could spit the slick, black seeds. The next spring, two-eared plants would sprout up in the grass. I always called Papa's attention to them so he'd transplant them to the garden.

"Can't grow melons here in Holladay," he'd say, shaking his head. "Frost comes too late in the spring and too early in the fall. Summer nights are too cool."

Would it be possible to harvest a melon crop in New Mexico? Enough to eat for breakfast, dinner, and supper? Could I really have all I wanted? It sounded too good to be true.

I picked up a stick and began to draw in the dirt, a whole row of watermelon smiles, one right next to the other. The pretty scalloped pattern forming on the ground started an idea itching in the back of my mind. Before I figured out the details, I heard Mama asking about the school.

"Don't worry," Papa assured her. "There will be one."

"And a church?"

"Probably lots of them," Papa said, laughing. "All kinds— Baptist, Presbyterian, Catholic . . . Take your pick."

"Oh, Albert," Mama said, "quit teasing me. You know I mean a Latter-day Saint Church."

"Yes, my dear," Papa replied seriously. "There's one right in Clovis."

"That's good," Mama said. "We'd be lost without our church."

"John Talbot is a member down there. That's why he offered the land to Clem and his friends—so they'd have a bigger congregation. But don't expect New Mexico to be like it is here in Utah. We Latter-day Saints will be greatly outnumbered down there. Even with twelve new families moving in, the group will be small."

I'd never thought about other churches before. Everyone I knew went to the same one, The Church of Jesus Christ of Latter-day Saints. We usually called ourselves Latter-day Saints or just plain Saints, but sometimes we were known as Mormons. Papa made sure we all knew that Mormon was only a nickname, however.

"It was first used as an insult by enemies of the church," he explained. "They claimed that we worship the man who compiled the *Book Of Mormon* instead of Jesus Christ."

"But that's not true," Mama added.

"*Mormon* has been used so much that it's not considered a bad word anymore," Papa said, "but it shows more respect for Christ if you don't use it."

So we didn't.

"Who else is going to New Mexico?" Mama asked Papa.

He mentioned some names I didn't know. "And the Lenstroms," he added.

"I'm glad of that," Mama said. "Elizabeth is my good friend. And Caroline and Dora will have Jenny and Sarah to play with."

While Mama and Papa talked more about moving, I scratched a picture of four girls playing hopscotch.

"Are all the families from Holladay?" Mama asked.

"Most of them, I think," Papa replied, "and maybe a couple of Clem's relatives from Cottonwood."

"How do we earn a homestead farm?" Mama wanted to know.

"I don't know all the specific rules," Papa said, "but we have to live in a house on the property and make the land productive. After five years, it's ours to keep."

"How will we manage until we can harvest a crop?" Mama wanted to know.

"We'll have to watch our pennies," Papa said, "but we're good at that. We'll grow our own food and do without what we can't afford to buy. I'll look for some bricklaying jobs when there's a lull in the farm work, like I do here. Homesteaders need chimneys the same as anyone else."

"Yes," Mama agreed. "Even in a warm, mild climate, we women have to cook."

"It will be nice not to shovel snow," Papa said.

No snow? No fox and geese games? No making angel wings or snowmen? No sleigh rides with bells jangling on the horses' harnesses? No hot spiced cider to warm us up afterward? I felt a hollow, empty place under my ribs, like the time I'd lost my lucky penny down a crack in the floor. Did I really want to leave Utah and go to New Mexico? For a minute, I wondered.

Still and all, to take the whole family and move to a different state where there would be room to grow watermelons seemed like such an exciting thing to do. I almost couldn't breathe just thinking about it. As soon as Ed got home from school he'd probably take me with him to tell our friends.

Mama finished the folding, and she and Papa both sat down

on the top step. They stayed there for a while, just thinking. Finally Mama spoke, and she asked exactly what I wanted to know.

"How far is it to Clovis, New Mexico?"

"Best I can figure from the map," Papa told her, "is about nine hundred miles."

"*Nine hundred miles!*" Mama gasped. "That's like the pioneers crossing the plains to Utah."

"Not quite," Papa assured her. "Only three fourths as far. We'll go in wagons, the same as they did, but we won't be blazing new trails. We'll travel on well-worn roads and pass through towns along the way to replenish our supplies. And best of all, there's already a house on the property. The move will be an adventure, not an ordeal."

"How long will it take?" Mama asked.

"Five or six weeks," Papa said, "as near as I can figure."

"That's a long trip," Mama observed.

"Yup," Papa agreed, "but October is the best time to go—not too hot, not too cold. We might be able to celebrate Thanksgiving on our own place this year."

"That would be nice," Mama said.

Just then George called out, "Howie's awake," and Mama went into the house. Papa came down the stairs, and I moved over to let him pass, but he sat down beside me instead.

"How about that, Dora?" he said. "Doesn't a homestead farm sound like a good idea?"

I smiled and bobbed my head up and down.

"I thought you'd think so," he said.

I pointed to my drawing in the dirt.

"That's a lot of watermelon," Papa said. "Do you think you can eat that much?"

I nodded *yes*.

"I don't doubt it." He laughed, gave me a hug, and headed for the barn.

I stayed on the step, waiting for Ed to get home from school. Until then, I had plenty to think about.

CHAPTER TWO

WORDLESS MESSAGES

Ithought about how much I wanted to be in the classroom. Ed was the only one who really knew how I felt about school, and he couldn't understand why anyone would *want* to go. He hated it.

Just this morning, I'd walked down to the schoolhouse with him.

"Life's not fair," he grumbled. "You want to go to school and I don't."

I nodded my agreement.

"Let's trade clothes," he suggested. "You can pretend to be me."

That silly idea made me smile. I waited with him until Miss Peterson came out and rang the bell. The other children hurried inside, but Ed didn't move a muscle until the teacher shook the bell again. At us. Finally, he shuffled through the door like a convict going to jail in leg irons. Then, the same as always, the teacher waved me off. No matter how quietly she closed the door behind her, I felt as if she had slammed it in my face.

While I waited for Ed to come home, I scratched a crooked door in the dirt, all out of kilter from being banged shut. Then I drew another door—an open one, the kind I intended to walk through someday.

My mind wanted to know things. What made the sky blue? Why was grass green? How could a little seed grow into a big plant?

It seemed to me that people's brains must be made out of different materials. Ed's and mine were as different as feathers and flypaper. His was flighty; mine was sticky. All the things that went into my head seemed to stay stuck in nice neat rows. If I concentrated, I could pick out an idea and think about it any time I wanted to.

Ed couldn't do that at all. Mama said everything she told him went in one ear and out the other. It made me think that his ears were like two open windows and the thoughts blew through like lazy feathers riding on a breeze, not touching his mind at all. I imagined all the things he heard in the classroom and didn't catch must be whirling around outside his head like puffs of goose down after a pillow fight. They'd float away and he'd never get them back. And he didn't even care.

Whenever I tried to get Ed to tell me about school or teach me to read, he said, "School's a pain in the neck. Forget it."

I couldn't forget it. I wanted to grab all those loose ideas and file them in my mind so they'd be handy if I ever learned to talk. Maybe the reason things stayed in my head so long was because they couldn't get out the usual way—through my mouth.

I drew some feathers flying in the air over the crooked door. They seemed to tickle the notion that was taking shape in my mind—the pattern for my sampler.

Just a week ago, I'd unwrapped my birthday present from Mama to find a rectangular piece of white cloth and twelve colors of embroidery thread.

I shrugged my shoulders to ask *What's it for?*

"For your sampler," Mama had explained. "A girl who can embroider as nicely as you do should make a sampler to show off all the different stitches she knows."

She pointed to the piece of framed embroidery over the couch.

"Like the one I made," she'd said. "Only yours doesn't have to say *HOME SWEET HOME*."

The words were stitched with fancy, flowery letters in all sorts of colors.

"You can use any pattern you like," Mama had continued. "I'll bet you can draw your own design."

I looked at the line of watermelon smiles in the dirt. They would make a perfect scalloped border—a green and rosy frame. I'd make the black seeds with French knots. After the edge was done, I'd figure out what to put in the center. Maybe the slammed door with floating feathers. Maybe the open door—if they let me go to school in New Mexico.

Just then Ed's shrill whistle split the air, signaling to me that he was on his way home. He ran ahead of Frank and Caroline, and I hurried off to meet him, skipping and smiling so he could tell I was happy about something.

"Good news?" he asked.

I grinned and bobbed my head up and down.

"Mama's making cookies?" he guessed.

I shook my head *no*.

"Papa gave you a penny to spend?"

I shook my head again.

"What, then?" he wanted to know.

I grabbed his hand and we ran up to the house. I pulled him to the place by the back step and showed him what I'd been drawing in the dirt. He scratched his head and tried to figure it out.

"Well," he said, "it looks like lots of pieces of watermelon."

I nodded my head rapidly.

He pointed to the out-of-shape door, "And a . . . ?"

I ran up the steps and patted the kitchen door.

"A door?"

I nodded.

"Why so crooked?"

I opened the door and slammed it shut with a loud bang.

He looked puzzled.

"A slammed door?" he asked.

I agreed with a fast bob of my head.

"So what does it mean?" he wanted to know.

I wanted to explain about moving to New Mexico where we'd have lots of watermelon, and maybe the schoolhouse door wouldn't be slammed, so I'd be able to learn to read and write.

I pointed at him and then me and tried to say, "Move to New Mexico." It came out more like "Mmoo Nnmmmo."

"What?" he said, puzzled.

"Mmoo, mmoo," I said louder.

"Cow?" he asked.

I shook my head and drew a team of horses.

"Horses," he said, "not cows."

I added a loaded-up wagon so he'd understand *move*.

"Oh, I get it!" he shouted, "we're going to haul the junk to the dump! Yippee! I'm gonna see if I can find another wheel to match the one I got last time." He was gone like a shot, calling to Papa.

"It's no use," I screamed silently to myself. "I can't make him understand. I can't tell anyone anything. Why can't I talk? Why can't I write? Why can't I go to school like everyone else? Why? It's not fair; it's just not fair!"

I plunged through the willow wall of my playhouse and banged my fists against the tree trunk.

The hurt was so deep, I cried for a long time. I cried until all the tears I had inside were squeezed out, and I felt like a dried-up, leftover lemon peel—until I was too tired to sob even one more time. The crying didn't change anything. I still couldn't talk. But my heart didn't feel quite as heavy anymore, as if part of the sadness had been washed away.

On Sunday, all the people at church were talking about the families who were going to move, and everyone was offering to help us. Mama hurried me off to my class, where my teacher was giving leather Bibles to the children who had had a hundred percent attendance for a year. She had a supply of black ones for the boys, white for the girls. I wanted one of those Bibles so badly I could hardly stand it. I'd had only three more weeks to go to earn one when I caught the chicken pox from Caroline, missed two Sundays in a row, and had to start at the beginning again. Now we'd be gone in less than a month. There was no way I could have such a beautiful book.

After the class, I went up to the front of the room to look at the one white Bible that was left. As I reached to touch it, Sister Johnson turned from taking down the pictures she'd pinned on the wall for the lesson. I quickly pulled my hand away. She looked at me with love in her eyes.

"You're moving away soon, aren't you, Dora?"

I nodded my head.

"I'll miss having you in my class," she said. "I can tell you're learning everything we talk about."

I nodded again.

"Would you like to have that Bible to take with you?" she asked.

I bobbed my head up and down so fast I could feel my curls bouncing, and she handed me the book. I hugged it tight against my heart and looked at her through watery eyes.

"You really love Jesus, don't you?"

I smiled my answer.

"Don't forget that He loves you, too," Sister Johnson said and stooped to take me in her arms. She squeezed me tight for a long time before she kissed the top of my head and patted my behind to send me on my way.

"Bless you, child," she whispered.

I skipped from the room so happy I wished I could sing. I did the best I could. I hummed a hymn.

Maybe in New Mexico, a kind teacher like Sister Johnson would let me go to school. I promised myself that whether one did or not, somehow I would learn to read the Bible and teach myself to write what I wanted to say. No matter how hard it was, I would do it.

CHAPTER THREE

SORTING AND PACKING

We had to leave less than a month after we found out about the homestead. There wasn't much time to get ready, and soon the whole family was busy sorting and packing.

Each day, I thought of all the things I'd miss when we were gone—mostly the people. Grandma and Grandpa and all the unmarried aunts and uncles lived in the big, white house just down the lane from our small, brown one. Grandpa had a herd of cows that his boys milked night and morning. They delivered the milk daily to his regular customers. Every morning, I went to get our own bucket filled, and usually stayed long enough to do some little jobs for Grandma.

"How about a cookie?" she'd offer. "Or would you rather have a slice of hot bread with honey?" I'd miss Grandma's treats and her floury hugs.

I'd miss Grandpa, too. He often came into our kitchen, sweating from working in the field.

"Do you have any of that good homemade root beer, Betty?" he'd ask Mama. I'd hurry down the basement stairs to get some for him.

"That sure hits the spot," he'd say, smacking his lips.

I'd be lonesome for the family of cousins who lived across the alfalfa field—especially Ilene, who was my best friend. I'd miss everyone else in my Sunday School class, too, except Jenny Lenstrom, of course. She was moving to New Mexico with us. All the children in that class were in the grade I should have been in at school.

"Next to our homes, the church is the most important part of a Latter-day Saint community," Papa said. "And the school is second. Usually they are built near each other in the center of town."

Ours were both close enough for us to walk to. Would they be that convenient in New Mexico?

While I thought about what I hated to leave, I had to decide which things I wanted to take. Papa had made a small wooden chest for my birthday.

"That's all the room you can have," he told me.

How could I fit the treasures I'd collected in my nine years of life into a space smaller than a bread box?

I folded my sampler into a neat, little packet with the embroidery thread, hoop, thimble, extra needles, and a tiny pair of scissors.

Mama had already marked the scalloped border of watermelon smiles around the edge. I set it aside to put on top of my other things, so I could get it out easily to work on while we traveled.

I packed and repacked the chest over and over again, but I never could get it to hold everything I wanted.

Mama and Papa were having the same problem with the wagon. "It just isn't big enough," Mama complained, "to take all we need and eight people besides."

"It will have to be," Papa told her. "We'll sell everything we don't have room for, and that'll give us some money to buy what we need when we get there. We can only take what we have to. The wagon itself will be our shelter."

"The bedsprings and mattress will fit across the wagon box," Mama said. "Quilts spread on top will make a soft place to ride in the daytime or sleep at night. We can pack lots of things underneath the bed."

Mama insisted that her stove had to go, too. She wasn't taking any chances about replacing it. "It takes too long to get used to a new one," she told Papa.

I knew the real reason she didn't want to go without it. I heard what she whispered when she took the bread pudding from the oven and it was baked to the perfect shade of golden brown. "Ah, dear and faithful friend," she told the stove. "You can cook anything just the way it ought to be done. I'm certainly not leaving you behind!"

We had to take food that wouldn't spoil. We packed cured hams and bacon, dried beans, cheese coated with wax; potatoes, parsnips, and onions; cornmeal, oatmeal, and cracked wheat for mush; flour, sugar, salt, and spices and some bottled fruit wrapped in newspapers so the jars wouldn't break.

"We'll be able to hunt wild game for fresh meat," Papa said, "and we'll take the cow Dad gave us so we'll have milk and butter."

Mama packed a few cooking utensils to use on the trip and some pie tins for plates. Papa promised her she could buy a new set of dishes in Clovis.

We filled kegs and crates, burlap bags, bushel baskets, and flour sacks. It was up to Papa to fit them all into the wagon box without wasting an inch of space.

Two days before we left, he and Mama were busy loading everything up. I sniffed the mixed smell of crisp canvas, new leather, and sawdust from freshly cut wood. Papa nailed boards across the wagon to hold the stove in place behind the driver's seat. He anchored the water barrels with leather straps and wedged boxes and bags wherever they fit.

Ilene sat by me on the step, watching me fill my wooden chest for the last time. It hadn't ever bothered her that I couldn't speak. No matter what game we played, she could keep up both ends of the conversation without hardly stopping to breathe. When she wanted to put on a play she had a different voice for every part, and all I had to do was help her act out the story. I was getting pretty good at pantomime. It helped me explain what I was trying to say.

I couldn't pretend I was happy when I wasn't, though. That day I could feel the sad sag in my face because I had to leave my good friend behind. My ear was aching, too. I didn't know why.

I remembered the time Jake Woodrow had called me Dumb Dora.

"Dumb Dora, dumb Dora, dumb, dumb, dumb," he chanted.

Ilene whipped out at him like a coiled-up rattlesnake.

"Dora's not dumb!" she hissed.

"Is too," he said. "Can't talk, can she?"

"Just because she can't talk doesn't mean she's dumb," Ilene yelled at him. "She has more brains in her little finger than you have in your whole head!" She dotted the exclamation point with a fist in his stomach.

With a gasp, Jake bent over double like a hairpin. He shot daggers of hate at her with his eyes, but he never called me Dumb Dora again.

"Will everything fit in your chest?" Ilene asked me. I shook my head and rearranged things again.

I placed the white leather Bible in the bottom. Pressed between its pages were a few beautiful red leaves I'd gathered from the bright maples growing behind Grandpa's farm at the foot of Mt. Olympus. I'd tied yarn both ways around the book so they wouldn't fall out.

Next, I dropped some seeds in a little crack that was left by the side of the Bible. There were eight brown beans, half a dozen watermelon seeds, and a handful of maple wings—some to plant and some to play with. They were shaped like long figure eights with one fat seed in each end. I loved the way they fell whirling to the ground when I tossed them in the air.

I tucked in the long strand of tiny glass beads I had strung at Sister Johnson's. She had given them to me in a slim bottle with a cork stopper one day when Mama was visiting her. While they talked, I had picked up the beads one at a time with a thin needle and slipped them along the thread, choosing the colors as I went.

I began to fold a doll shawl small enough to fit in the other end of the box. Then I changed my mind. I had made the coverlet myself from Mama's yarn scraps when I first learned to crochet, and it was soft and warm and cuddly. I handed it to Ilene.

"For keeps?" she asked, and I nodded my head *yes*. She hugged it and tickled her cheek with the fringe, and her eyes looked the same way mine felt—sort of wet and shiny.

"Will the doll fit?" she wanted to know. I answered by placing Henrietta on a soft place I'd made with her flannel nightie. Henrietta was a beautiful painted-eye doll with a china head and hands and a stuffed-leather body. Some girls had shut-eye dolls, but I wouldn't have traded because I loved Henrietta so much. I wrapped my little mirror in an old, blue sweater so it wouldn't break and tucked it in the box with a couple of doll dresses. Next went my paper pad and a pencil for drawing more designs and, last of all, the sampler. That was all the chest would hold.

"What about these?" Ilene asked, pointing to the rest of my treasures beside her on the step. I shook my head and handed them to her, one by one—an old hat and a pair of shoes we used to play dress-up, some more doll clothes and a raggedy fairy-tale book. When I came to the bag of marbles, I dumped them out in my lap, selected five or six of my favorites, and pushed them into the corners of my box. I returned the rest to the bag and gave it to my friend.

After Ilene went home with her arms full, I watched Mama hand a bushel basket to Papa to put in the wagon.

"Where do you think is the best place for the chickens?" she asked.

"Chickens?" Papa groaned. "We're not taking any chickens."

"Of course we are," Mama insisted. "Three or four of the best layers and Caroline's pet rooster so we can raise chicks in the spring. And some stewing hens to eat on the way."

Papa sighed. When Mama had that determined sound in her voice, he knew it was no use to argue. Besides, chicken dinner was his favorite.

"I guess we can put them in a crate and tie it to the side by the wash tubs. You'd better get some chicken feed."

"It's already packed," she assured him. "Will we have plenty of water?"

"We're taking two barrels," Papa told her, "one for drinking, one for washing. We'll fill them when we need to. No use hauling the extra weight if we're by a stream."

The pain in my ear was crawling down the side of my neck. It had started two or three days before as a tender spot. Now it was a sore and throbbing lump. I showed it to Ed.

"That's quite a bump," he said. "You better tell Mama about it."

"Oh, my, that's bad," Mama said and felt my forehead. "You're burning up with fever. Albert," she called to Papa, "come look at this."

He did.

"It's a great big boil," he said, "nearly popping with pus. We better take her to the doctor. If it were anywhere else, I'd lance it myself, but infections anywhere on the head are dangerous. They could drain into the brain."

The doctor? The very word scared me. No one in our family had ever been to a doctor as long as I could remember. It cost too much money. Papa took care of all the sick children and animals by himself. Luckily, we were healthy most of the time.

"What will the doctor do?" Ed wanted to know.

"Cut it open and drain out the pus," Papa told him.

"Will it hurt?" Ed asked.

"Probably will for a minute or two," Papa said, "but after that it will feel better."

I didn't like the idea of having any part of me cut open, even if it would quit hurting afterward. I ran out into the orchard to hide.

After a while, Papa found me.

"Come on, Dora," he coaxed kindly. "You really need to go to the doctor."

I shook my head.

"We can't start on our trip until that boil's taken care of," he said, putting an arm around me and guiding me back toward the house.

Mama waited on the seat of the nearly loaded wagon. The horses were already hitched up. Papa boosted me up next to Mama.

"I'll let you two off at the doctor's while I go get the wagon cover," he said. He picked up the reins and clucked "let's go" to the horses.

A few minutes later, he pulled to a stop at a house that had a sign hanging by the front door. Papa handed Mama some money to pay the bill. He looked at it so long before he gave it to her that I could tell he hated to spend it.

After a short talk with Mama, the doctor took a look behind my ear.

"You're right," he told her. "It's an ugly boil in a bad place. I'll have to lance it." He picked up a small knife with a sharp point. When I pulled away he instructed Mama to hold my head still.

"This will just feel like a little pin prick," he explained. "It will be over before you can say 'Jack Robinson.'"

Right when he said the name, I felt the prick and then a warm stream running down my neck. He mopped it up with a piece of cotton. I looked at the yellow goo.

"There, now," he said, "that wasn't so bad, was it?"

I wanted to say, "Bad enough," but couldn't, of course, so I said nothing.

"Cat got your tongue?" he teased me.

I shook my head.

"She can't talk," Mama told him.

"Can't talk? Why not?"

"Don't know," Mama said.

The doctor looked into my mouth to see if he could tell what was wrong.

"Why, she's tongue-tied," he said.

"What's that?" Mama wanted to know. "I never heard of it."

"I'll show you," the doctor said, and Mama looked in my mouth, too.

"See how her tongue is fastened down?" He poked at it with a flat stick. "It's sealed along the bottom so she can't lift it at all."

"It looks like it's stuck with glue," Mama said. "I can't believe I've never noticed that."

"It's easy to miss," the doctor assured her.

"But think of all the times I fed her and didn't even look," Mama said. "How could I be so stupid?" Her voice was heavy with guilt.

"Don't be so hard on yourself," the doctor said. "Think about it. Every time you put a spoon in her mouth, it covered up her tongue. It was the same as with any of your other children. The only way to find a tied tongue is to know what you are looking for."

"And we didn't know," Mama said sadly.

"No, of course not," the doctor agreed. "But it surely explains why Dora can't talk. Her tongue needs to be free to move about to make the sounds of speaking. Otherwise no one can tell what the poor girl is trying to say."

"He's right about that," I thought.

"It's a very simple procedure to correct the problem," the doctor said.

"Really?" Mama asked.

"Really," the doctor assured her. He turned toward me.

"All I have to do is clip underneath your tongue so it isn't stuck down," he said. "Once it's loose, you'll be able to talk like anyone else."

I couldn't believe it. It looked like the hope I'd had all my life was finally going to be answered, all because I had an awful boil on my neck. At last I'd be able to talk!

"When would be a good time for the operation?" the doctor asked Mama.

"You'd better do it now," she said. "We're leaving on Monday."

CHAPTER FOUR

VERY SEVERE CASE

Fixing my tongue may have seemed like an easy thing to the doctor, but as far as I was concerned, it wasn't as simple as it sounded.

"First of all," he told me, "climb up on the table and lie down."

I did.

"Now, open wide," the doctor continued, "while I drop some ether on your tongue to make it numb so you won't feel anything."

He unscrewed the lid of a small jar, sucked up some liquid in an eye dropper, and drizzled it on my tongue. It felt freezing cold at first. It smelled sickly sweet and tasted terrible.

Before long my mouth felt like it had gone to sleep, and my head was woozy.

"You'll need to hold her still while I operate," the doctor told Mama, placing her hands on opposite sides of my head and pushing them tight.

The room seemed to spin in a foggy blur, and I started to feel numb all over. He was right. I couldn't feel anything while he clipped my tongue loose.

Occasionally, during the operation, I woke up a little and heard some faraway voices talking. The only words I remembered were "very severe case."

I felt wide awake by the time the doctor wiped the blood off my face and helped me down from the table. My mouth didn't hurt at all.

"Such a brave young lady deserves to have a piece of candy to suck on to get rid of that awful ether taste," he said, pulling a coin from his pocket.

"Go to the store and pick out your favorite kind," he said, handing me the money.

A nickel. A whole nickel! I'd never had more than a penny to spend for candy before. I tried to say "thank you," now that I could talk. Nothing happened. My tongue didn't move. I couldn't even feel it.

What was wrong? Had the doctor made a mistake? I touched his sleeve and pointed in my mouth.

"Still numb?" he asked. "Don't worry, that will soon wear off."

After Mama paid the doctor, I pulled her across the street to the store. I wanted to buy the biggest stick of peppermint I could. I wouldn't have to share it with anyone or nibble it slowly to make it last. I'd have enough to go right ahead and chew it up.

I traded my nickel for a fat stick of candy striped with red and white. As soon as I took one big bite, I could tell there was something wrong. It didn't crack between my teeth the way it should. It felt kind of tough and leathery and had sort of a salty taste, like when I sucked my finger after a cut. I had forgotten how peppermint can sting, and it burned like fire, especially where the doctor had clipped under my tongue.

I wanted to spit it out and I felt the juice dribbling down my chin. I tugged at Mama's sleeve to ask for a handkerchief. When she turned to see what I wanted, she gasped.

"What happened, Dora? You're bleeding again!" The numbness was wearing off now, and my tongue hurt. The pain got worse and worse.

Mama rushed me back to the doctor. After he looked in my mouth, he said, "Oh, dear, she's chewed her tongue. It looks like a piece of raw meat. Didn't I warn you about that?"

"No," Mama said in a voice made of ice. "You didn't." I wondered if she was going to ask for her money back.

"Well, she's learned the hard way," the doctor said. Then he explained to me what had happened.

"Most people learn how to keep their tongues away from their teeth from the beginning, but yours was tied down where it wasn't in any danger. Now that it's cut loose, it can easily get between those sharp choppers. Unless you are very careful, you will bite it." Then he asked Mama, "Do you have any ice?"

He meant, Did we have any ice left in our icehouse from last winter, or had it all melted?

"More than we need," Mama assured him. "Albert always packs it in plenty of sawdust."

"Then give her some ice chips to suck on to keep the swelling down," the doctor said. "And remember," he continued, pointing his finger at me, "that I said *suck*, not chew. I believe that's what I said about the candy, too."

When he mentioned it, I remembered that he had.

"You should rinse your mouth out with warm salt water several times a day," he told me.

The very thought of salt water on my sore tongue made me cringe. I knew how much a tiny bit of salt could hurt a cut finger, and I had no intention of using it in my tender mouth.

The doctor handed Mama some pills to give me for the pain.

"You'd better take one now," he said, and handed me a glass of water. "Stick with soft food for a day or two and be careful of that tongue when you eat."

Just then Papa came back to pick us up.

"Did the boil get lanced?" he asked as we climbed into the wagon.

I nodded my head *yes*. I'd almost forgotten why we'd come to the doctor in the first place.

"But that's not the most important thing," Mama began. She talked nonstop all the way home, telling him exactly what had happened. She finished with, "And now her tongue's cut loose but it hurts worse than the boil did," and Papa had a chance to speak.

"So," he said, giving me a squeeze, "dear little Dora is going to learn to be a jabberbox, is she? That is good news."

"It won't be easy," Mama predicted, "but if anyone can do it, Dora can."

As soon as the rest of the family heard about my operation,

they expected me to speak immediately. I had expected that, too. But it didn't happen. After chewing my tongue, I wasn't going to try moving it at all. I was partly mad about it, partly sad, and a whole lot disappointed.

"Dora's tongue is too sore for talking so soon," Mama explained to the others. She told them what had happened with the peppermint.

Ed must have noticed the tears brimming in my eyes. He tried to get me to think about something else.

"Have you figured out what's the first thing you're going to say?" he asked.

I shook my head.

"'Hallelujah! I can talk!'" Caroline suggested.

"'Please pass the peas,'" Frank said.

"'Now I can go to school!'" Ed guessed.

What *would* I say first? I'd never thought about that.

"The most important thing right now," Papa said, "is to get Dora's tongue healed up so she can say anything. I'll go get some ice chips."

Mama had the saltwater rinse ready in a minute, and even though I shook my head, she insisted that I use it. Just as I expected, it stung worse than the peppermint. The cold ice chips felt good after that.

"What you need is some nice warm broth," Mama said. "I'll kill one of those chickens we don't have room to take and make some for you."

She had to cook it at Grandma's because everything in our kitchen was either packed, sold, or given away. When the clear soup was done, she placed a steaming bowl in front of me.

"This will do you good," she said. "It will flow right under your sore tongue and the heat will help heal the cut."

I wouldn't even try the golden liquid.

"No salt," Mama promised, "and nothing to chew."

Cautiously I dipped out a spoonful and blew it cool enough that it didn't burn. The first sip tasted pretty good, and I had some more. It did make my hollow stomach feel better. I finished the whole bowlful.

By now, everything was loaded in the wagon except the table and chairs.

"We can't take them," Papa said. "There's just no more room."

"Oh, Albert," Mama cried, "we can't get along without a place to eat."

"I know, hon," he agreed. "I promise I'll make some new ones as soon as we get there."

I noticed Mama held her lips together tight, like she was afraid she might say something she'd be sorry for. Then she straightened her shoulders as if she were getting ready to carry a heavy load.

For the first time, I wondered if she really wanted to move.

CHAPTER FIVE

BUT WITH JOY, WEND YOUR WAY

The next day, after all our church meetings, we had a good-bye dinner at Grandma's house with all the aunts, uncles, and cousins. While I sipped more warm chicken broth, everyone else had a feast. Except for roast pork instead of turkey, it was just like Thanksgiving. I remembered what Papa had said about maybe having Thanksgiving dinner at our own place in New Mexico this year. Feeling sad, I counted all the people who would be missing if we did.

After the kitchen table was cleared, Papa pulled out the map

Brother Coldwell had given him and showed all of us the route we'd take.

"We'll leave from the church at eight o'clock tomorrow morning," he said, "and head west to Murray." Papa's finger followed a red line across the page from right to left, turned the corner, and continued down the page. "Then south on the main road until we get to Spanish Fork. From there, we'll follow the Old Spanish Trail southeast through Price, Green River, Moab, and Monticello. After that, we'll cut across the corner of Colorado into New Mexico."

The next day, when the members of our wagon train assembled, Brother Coldwell made sure the men had their maps. He explained the rules of the trail, divided the daily duties, and assigned each family a place in line. Since he was in charge of the company, the Coldwell wagon would lead. The Lenstroms' would be second in line and ours, third.

Brother Coldwell introduced the two men who were chosen to ride ahead as scouts. They would check the road, locate our camping sites, and hunt for game when we needed meat.

"We won't hold regular church services while we travel," our leader explained. "But we'll all have morning and evening prayers together."

I knew some of the men prayed so long it seemed like a Sunday sermon.

All of our relatives were there to see us off. Grandma hugged each of us again and again and kept wiping her eyes with a handkerchief. It seemed like a time to say something important, but no one said much. Papa noted the date on his map. Monday, October 3, 1910.

Ilene stood close to me, holding her doll wrapped in the shawl

I'd given her. She pressed something smooth and round into my hand. It was her favorite rock. "Keep it . . . " she choked out, " . . . for good luck." For once, she was at a loss for words.

Travelers and well-wishers all stood in a circle to have a final prayer together before we left. Almost everyone had tears shining in their eyes when *Amen* was whispered at the end. Nearby, two rowdy boys were making such a loud racket that I hoped they weren't going with us.

I was glad I already knew how to keep my mouth shut when I was excited. That's the only way I could be sure not to chew on my tongue again. It was still plenty sore from the day before, but didn't feel quite as swollen. It hurt to move it, so I held it still. I kept thinking of things I wanted to say, but trying to talk was out of the question.

As we headed toward the wagons, Brother Lenstrom's fiddle screeched a long sigh and his deep voice boomed:

> *Come, come, ye Saints,*
> *No toil or labor fear,*
> *But with joy, wend your way . . .*

Everyone in the assembly knew this Mormon pioneer hymn and the message of hope in the final lines, "All is well, All is well."

The song passed from one person to the next until we all joined in. I noticed that Brother Lenstrom skipped right over the verse that said, "And should we die before our journey's through." In an extra-loud voice, he started at the beginning again.

By then, most of the sadness at leaving was gone, and we waved our last good-byes, happy to be on our way. I breathed a sigh of relief that the two rowdy boys were still scuffling on the ground. Apparently they would not be part of the company. At the last minute, though, they both jumped up onto the wagon behind us.

"The Brownleys," Papa said, shaking his head.

As our caravan of twelve wagons started off in a line, I felt like we were part of the Pioneer Day Parade held every year on the Twenty-Fourth of July. People came out of their houses and waved as we passed.

After we got to Murray, we drove straight down State Street, past the towns of Sandy, Midvale, and Jordon. Then the road had to turn right to swing around the point of the mountain. The sun was setting when we approached the next town, Lehi.

Papa said, "Tonight we'll be able to enjoy the way members of our church take care of each other even when they aren't personally acquainted."

"Why, what's the plan?" Mama wanted to know.

"When the Lehi Relief Society ladies heard we were coming, they decided to fix enough food to feed us all," Papa told her. "We'll camp overnight on the church lot and they'll bring breakfast, too."

The roast beef and pan-browned potatoes looked and smelled so good that I wanted to gobble them up the way everyone else did. But my mouth was still too sore to try chewing yet. Mama gave me an extra big serving of the smooth, nutmeg-flavored custard that was one of the desserts. It slid easily over my sore tongue and tasted delicious.

The second night, we were invited to another home-cooked meal, in Spanish Fork. It was brought to our campground by church members and served around a big bonfire. New friendships formed quickly. Before the evening was over, our family became acquainted with the Jensens. It seemed as if we'd known them all our lives when they asked our family to come to their house for breakfast in the morning.

"That's all the pampering we're going to get," Papa said the next day, as he mopped up elderberry syrup with his last bite of pancake. "Here's where we turn off the main road onto the Old Spanish Trail. After we cross the mountains, towns are few and far between in the wide-open spaces of eastern Utah."

Papa pulled the map out of his pocket and reviewed the names again. Price, Green River, Moab, and Monticello.

Papa tapped a spot on the map south of Monticello. "Here's the only place in the United States where four states meet," he said. "Utah, Colorado, New Mexico, and Arizona all have one corner in common. There are lots of Indian reservations in this area."

"Indians?" Mama gasped.

"Indians!" Ed exclaimed.

"We might see some," Papa said.

"I hope not!" Mama said at exactly the same time Ed said, "I hope we do!"

"Don't worry," Papa assured Mama. "They won't be any trouble."

"I'd just as soon not meet any at all," Mama told him.

Just then, Brother Jensen brought another plate of pancakes, but everyone was too full to eat any more.

"How long will it take us to get to Price from here?" Papa asked him.

"About six or seven days," Brother Jensen said. "My brother lives in Price and we go over to visit once in a while, but it's a hard trip. The road over Soldier Summit is pretty steep in some places— especially going down into Helper. You'll pass through some other little mining towns, too, but no place you'll want to stop."

"Why not?" Mama wanted to know.

"Too much smoking, drinking, and gambling for Latter-day Saints to feel comfortable. It's better to find your own campgrounds until you get to Price. You'll find lots of church members to welcome you there."

It sounded to me like people from our church were more at home with each other than with anyone else. I wondered how we'd get along in New Mexico, with all those other churches down there.

We stood up from the table and headed back to the wagon.

After the horses were hitched up, Papa asked Mama, "Are we ready for a week of camping out? This is our last chance for a long while to get any supplies."

"I wish we had some apples," Mama said.

Just at that moment, like a genie in a bottle making her wish come true, Brother Jensen came across the lot carrying a bushel of rosy Jonathans.

"I thought your children might like something juicy to chew on," he said, lifting the basket into the back of the wagon. He turned to Papa.

"Do you think you'd have room to take another bushel to my brother's family in Price?" he asked.

"Of course we would," Papa told him and leaned into the wagon to see where we could put one more basket.

Both bushels had to sit on top of the bed. It made us crowded when all of us children rode, but usually some of us were walking. It was easy to reach for a crunchy apple whenever we wanted one.

Just the thought of the tart, juicy, goodness made my mouth

water. The prospect of chewing apples, though, reminded me of the peppermint stick. I held my mouth shut tight. Finally, I broke an apple in half and sucked the delicious juice. It tasted so good that I scraped off tiny bits with my teeth and swallowed them without chewing.

The sunny autumn days were beautiful—brisk and cool in the morning so that everyone was eager to start moving, and warm enough in the afternoon to make the younger children drowsy.

We took turns riding with Papa on the driver's seat. From there we could look at everything that was up ahead. When we rode in the back of the wagon we couldn't see anything until we'd passed it, or, if the canvas sides were rolled up, we could look sideways. Sometimes we walked along behind with Betsy, the cow. Sometimes we ran ahead to the Lenstrom wagon.

The third day out of Spanish Fork, it was George's and my turn to be in front with Papa. Already the country looked different from the Salt Lake Valley. What had happened to the high, rocky mountains like the ones that stood guard over our home in Holladay? And where was the heavy growth of aspens and pines we had in our canyons? What made the dirt the color of rusty nails? I had so many questions I needed to ask. I pointed around, hoping Papa could figure out what I wanted to know.

"Sure is good deer country," he told me, as he followed my finger with his eyes. "Wouldn't be surprised if our scouts bring in some deer meat for supper one of these nights."

The cottonwoods growing along the stream glistened like gold in the Indian-summer sunlight. We were close to a railroad track and often passed long trains going the opposite way, loaded with black lumps of coal.

"From the mines in Price," Papa told me. "It's the biggest coal-mining center in the state."

We counted the cars together, Papa and George naming the numbers out loud, me just saying them in my mind. My tongue was not quite as sore as before. Soon I would be speaking the numbers myself. We waved at the man who looked at us out the window behind the engine.

When we stopped at night, the wagons were pulled into a safe, tight circle surrounding the campfires.

It was lucky for me that the last minute before we left home I had grabbed my jump rope from a nail behind the back door. It was like a strand of golden magic, it made so much difference in the way the other children treated me. By now, all of them had heard about my tongue operation. No one expected me to talk with a sore mouth, and they found out I didn't need to. Even Caroline was glad to know me.

As soon as the wagons were parked, the girls came shouting, "My turn with the jump rope, Dora!"

"No, it's mine," someone else would challenge, while we yanked up the dry weeds to clear a playing place. I tried to pull up sagebrush, but it was anchored like cement!

"I'll let you have a cookie," Martha bargained. She always carried cookies to barter for an early turn. Since she couldn't jump very long anyway, she usually found someone willing to trade. When it was decided which two girls would turn the rope and which one could jump first, the rest began to chant,

> *Mo-ther Hub-bard sat on a pin.*
> *How many inch-es did it go in?*
> *One, two, three, four . . . .*

As long as the jumper didn't miss a beat, it was her turn. If she jumped past twenty the others began to call out,

> *Ma-ble, Ma-ble, set the ta-ble,*
> *And don't for-get the*
> RED HOT PEPPER!

At this signal the rope started whirring at double time. No one could jump forever on red hot pepper, but I could last the longest!

While we waited to take our turns, we clapped and chanted together. No one noticed that one voice was missing from the refrain. I wanted to capture the happy moments and keep them forever. In my mind, I drew girls in cross-stitch dresses to embroider on my sampler.

While the girls jumped rope and played hopscotch, the boys did whatever Bradford Brownley dictated. He shouted out orders as if they were bullets. He aimed them at one boy and then another. No one had a chance to argue because Benjamin repeated everything his brother said. He sounded like an echo bouncing back in a canyon.

The men gathered brush and some bits of coal along the railroad to make the campfires. Then they milked the cows and fed the stock while the women unpacked their heavy skillets and Dutch ovens to cook supper.

After evening prayers, the children were put to bed and the grown-ups danced. From the place under the wagon where we older ones slept, we could watch them whirl in a fast polka or line up for the Virginia Reel, while Brother Lenstrom played his fiddle.

"We're just like the old-time pioneers," Ed reminded me.

CHAPTER SIX

BABY TALK

Papa kept track of the trip by studying his map and making notes in his journal. He wrote dates, distances, and descriptions. I kept track of the number of days with my sampler and remembered the places where I made progress with my speech.

Gradually my mouth began to heal. Bit by bit and bite by bite, I worked at teaching my tongue to stay where it belonged to avoid the sharp edges of my teeth. It would be time to start talking soon, but I wasn't quite ready yet.

I'd thought a lot about Ed's question: What would I say first? My initial words should be important, and I wanted to be sure they were pronounced correctly.

I wished I could be alone somewhere to practice talking in private. I wanted to hear what the words sounded like before I spoke to anyone else. There's no place to be by yourself in a covered wagon. Even when you think you are alone, you find out you're not.

Each afternoon, while the younger children napped, I leaned against an apple basket and embroidered a watermelon smile on my sampler. I had decided to complete one every day so I'd know how long it took us to get to New Mexico.

One day while I sewed, all the boys were asleep, even Ed. Caroline was riding up front. I warmed up my tongue to talk by shifting it around. It felt strange to be able to move it into any part of my mouth—to the roof, to the floor, into each cheek. I could even stick it out in front, the way Ed did when he was being sassy. I stretched it up almost to my nose and down toward my chin. It went from side to side easily.

I quietly dug the mirror out of my chest to see what my tongue looked like. I'd never thought to inspect it before. It was sort of rough on the top with a crack down the middle and streaky, stripey on the bottom when I lifted it up.

"Doesn't that hurt your tongue?" Ed whispered.

Startled that he was awake, I shook my head.

"Is it all better?" he asked.

I shrugged a *sort of.*

"Can you talk then?"

I shook my head *NO!*

Ed closed his eyes and said no more. Neither did I.

It seemed strange that as much as I wanted to speak, I was afraid to try it. What if the words came out all wrong? What if no one could understand me?

I knew the Brownley brothers would never let me forget any mistake I might make. Although other people didn't expect me to talk until my tongue healed, those bratty boys teased me about it almost every day.

Bradford always began. "Dumb Dora, dumb Dora, cat got your tongue, Dora?"

As soon as Bradford finished, Benjamin echoed. "Dumb Dora, dumb Dora, dumb, dumb, dumb."

Dumb Dora. Why did everyone seem to think those two words belonged together?

The Brownleys were ten times as bad as Jake Woodrow had been back in Holladay. How I wished Ilene were here with her quick fists to punch them both in the stomach!

I was so disgusted with them that I didn't even care when Bradford nearly got himself killed by a team of horses a couple of days later.

After traveling uphill for a long time in Spanish Fork Canyon, we'd finally reached Soldier Summit, the top of the mountain range we were crossing over into eastern Utah. We'd camped overnight before starting down the other side, heading toward Price. Ed and I were up front with Papa. The road was steep. Very steep.

As soon as we came to a wide enough place, Papa pulled off to the side, jerked on the brake, and yelled, "Whoa!" to the horses. After the wagon stopped, he jumped down and rolled a rock under each front wheel.

"All of you need to get out and walk now," he said, sweat

dripping off his face. We have to lighten the load or the wagon will run right over the horses."

Almost everyone in the company walked part of each day. This was the first time all of us needed to do it at the same time.

"Should we get behind and pull back?" Ed asked.

"That's what it needs," Papa agreed, "but it's too dangerous."

"*They're* doing it," Ed said, pointing to the Brownleys. Benjamin and Bradford were tugging at the tailgate, trying to slow the forward progress of their wagon.

Just then Bradford's boot hit a stone and his feet shot out from under him. He sat down with a plop and was dragged on the seat of his pants.

"Stop!" he screamed, trying to get to his feet. "Stop! Stop!" Benjamin repeated.

The wagon kept going. Bradford finally let go of the tailgate and dropped with a thud onto the rocky road. The horses from the wagon behind nearly ran over him before he rolled out of the way.

"Phew!" Ed said, "that was close."

"Serves him right!" I thought.

"Like I said," Papa remarked, shaking his head, "that's a dangerous way to slow down a wagon. Bradford's lucky he didn't get more than a hole in his pants."

Papa instructed all of us to walk along the edge of the road. "And watch your step," he added.

Mama held tightly to George's hand and Caroline and I traded off carrying Howie.

Walking down that steep hill with my baby brother in my arms, I realized that he was learning to talk. For a long time he'd been making gurgling and cooing noises and, now, all of a sudden, he was saying "Mu-mu, Pa-pa, mooooo." When he patted my face and said "Do-wah," I was pleased, but I was also ashamed of myself. It embarrassed me that a baby could do what I didn't dare try.

Everyone made a big fuss about how darling he was. Because he was just a baby, the way he talked was cute.

I knew everyone in the family was just as anxious to have *me* talk, but I surely didn't want them to make a big fuss when I did. I just wanted to talk in sentences like everyone else my age, naturally and easily, like I'd been doing it forever.

I didn't know how to begin, though. If I started the way Howie did, I'd sound like a baby, and that would give bullies like the Brownleys something else to tease me about. No nine-year-old girl likes to be called a baby.

The more I considered it, though, the more I figured out that Howie's method might be the only way. I wished he could show me, right now, while he was doing it, in some secret place where no one could hear the mistakes I might make. I thought about that a lot, and finally I knew what I had to do.

Howie always needed to be watched while Mama cooked supper over the campfire. Usually Caroline was in charge of him because she was the oldest. Once in a while, though, I tended him.

"He's a handful," Mama admitted. "He only knows one speed—fast. Ever since he learned to walk, he's been running."

I decided that I should be the one to take care of the baby. While everyone else was busy working or playing, I could study how he moved his mouth to make different sounds. Then I'd try them out.

That night I took Howie from Caroline and handed her my jump rope to share with the other girls.

As usual, the baby wiggled and squirmed until I set him on the ground. As soon as his feet touched the earth, he took off like a chicken chased by a cat, jabbering as he went.

"How can I get him to slow down enough for me to watch his lips?" I asked myself as I followed him between the clumps of sagebrush.

"If I get him tired enough, maybe he'll calm down," I decided.

I continued to chase him, waving my arms when he looked back to laugh at me.

Finally I pounced, and rolled him playfully on the ground. He kicked and wiggled. I tickled. He giggled.

"Mu-mu, Pa-pa, Do-wah," he said.

"Do-wah," I imitated him, pointing to myself. "Do-wah, Do-wah," I repeated.

Without even thinking about it, I had said my first word, "Do-wah." My own name. That was important enough, but the "r" was missing.

Howie laughed and chattered while I watched where his tongue went and imitated what he did. Soon I was making more of his sounds.

"Mu-mu. Pa-pa. Ma-ma."

Talking baby talk to a baby is okay. Howie loved it.

It was hard work, though, to make my tongue move as fast as his did. Before long it was tired. "I may not be tongue-tied," I thought, "but I'm tongue-tired." Howie was still babbling like he'd never run out of steam.

When the dinner bell rang, I hummed one tune after another all the way back to camp.

"You sound happy today," Mama said when we sat down to eat.

"Umhmm," I hummed.

"Your mouth must feel better."

I nodded.

"Can you talk then?" Ed wanted to know.

I shook my head hard and looked at Mama. I could tell she understood that I didn't want to be asked that question yet.

"Why not?" Caroline demanded.

"She's not ready to," Mama told them. "And," she added emphatically, "I don't want anyone bothering her about it until she is. Do you understand?"

Caroline and Ed both nodded that they did. At that instant, I knew the first sentence I wanted to say was, "I love Mama."

CHAPTER SEVEN

MY SURPRISE

For the first time since Spanish Fork, we stopped in a good-sized town—Price.

"This is a bustling coal center," Papa told us. "There are lots of miners and railroad people who aren't members of our church, as well as many who are."

Our scouts had ridden ahead, located the Latter-day Saint chapel and obtained permission for our wagon train to camp on the empty lot next to it.

"I need to find the Jensens to deliver some apples," Papa told

Brother Coldwell. "We may spend the night there, but we'll be back in time for prayers in the morning."

The Jensen family was pleased to have the fruit and eager to hear about their relatives in Spanish Fork. Sister Jensen invited us to park our wagon by the barn, have dinner with them, and spend the night in real beds for a change. By morning, we'd become good friends.

Before we left, I found Papa cutting some green reeds that were growing in a nearby marsh.

"What are you going to do with those?" Mama asked when he came back carrying a big bundle.

"Take 'em along," Papa said.

"What for?" Mama asked, shaking her head at the idea.

"Don't know exactly," Papa said. "But I'll think of something. It's not easy to find such nice reeds, and I couldn't pass them up."

"We could make baskets," Caroline said.

"Yep," Papa agreed, "or weave some seats for the new chairs."

Mama warmed up at the mention of chairs.

"Where can you put them?" she asked. "The wagon's full."

"I'll tie 'em on top," he said.

He did, and we hurried away to join the other wagons.

Each day, I learned new sounds from Howie. "Boo, oops, no, i–yi–yi." His mouth stretched wide like a yawn to say "aw." "G–g–g" stayed deep in his throat. I copied what he did and was careful to do it where no one else could hear. When I had a chance, I practiced moving my mouth silently to make the words I'd learned.

We traveled for several days through hot, dry desert, and then, right in the middle of nowhere, we came to the bustling town of

Green River. Or maybe it should be called a city. Papa said it was *cosmopolitan*.

"What's that?" Ed asked.

"All kinds of people from all kinds of places, doing all kinds of things," Papa explained.

It seemed like he was right. Trains came and went carrying people, cattle, coal, and ore. Stockyards were full of steers waiting to be shipped to market. New brick stores were going up on Main Street. Foreign-looking people with different styles of clothes mingled with familiar men, women, and children on the busy streets. I heard many strange words.

I poked Papa and pointed to an elegant three-story building with pointed gables. In front, water shot up in fancy fountains. It was by far the biggest and prettiest building we'd seen on our trip.

"The sign says it's the Palmer House Hotel," Papa told me. "Shall we take a look inside?"

"Umhmm," I agreed, nodding vigorously. Papa said, "Whoa," to the horses and pulled back on the reins. Coldwell's and Lenstrom's wagons were already stopped ahead of us.

Mama had a list of things she needed to buy.

"Caroline can go shopping with me," she told Papa, "if you'll show the sights to the rest of the family."

"I'd enjoy that," Papa said, lifting Howie to his shoulders and taking George by the hand.

After we looked around outside the Palmer House, we went inside. I'd never seen so many beautiful things: Thick rugs bloomed with fancy garden patterns. Soft sofas and elegant chairs were arranged in groups, where people sat visiting. Shiny tables held electric lamps or huge vases of flowers.

We didn't stay long. The minute Papa set Howie on the floor,

George wiggled away and the two youngsters raced through the room, grabbing sweets from the candy dishes and climbing on the furniture.

"Boys, boys," Papa cried, "don't touch!"

He caught Howie just as he started up the staircase. Ed and Frank cornered George and we got out of there as fast as we could.

Howie kicked and screamed, "No, no, no!"

He said *NO!* a lot lately and Mama blamed it on his age.

Next, Papa took us to see the new three-span bridge that was being built across the Green River.

"Too bad we didn't come six weeks later," he said.

"Why?" Frank wanted to know.

"We could cross the river on the bridge. The sign says it will be open December tenth."

"How do we get across now?" Ed asked.

"Drive through the water," Papa said. "The river is really shallow this time of year. In the spring when the water is high, people use the ferryboats." Papa pointed to them anchored nearby.

Whenever we camped for the night, Papa pulled out the map. He wrote the date and marked how far we'd traveled. It always amazed me that such a long day made such a short mark on the page. The line on the map didn't tell anything at all about whether the road went up or down or what kind of country we were traveling through. Or how hot it was getting. It seemed like Fourth-of-July weather, not at all like October.

Almost all the mountains we'd seen for several days were far away and flat on top. Mama called them *mesas*. No trees grew anywhere. The grass was sparse and dry. Traveling became tedious. Every day I looked forward to my time alone with Howie after the wagon train stopped for the night. We had fun together learning to talk.

But I had a problem. Howie couldn't make the "l" sound, so I couldn't either. The best I could do was, "I wuv Mama." I intended to say my first sentence correctly or not at all.

Almost as if she sensed what I needed, Mama started singing La–la–la songs to Howie. They were the same tunes as her go-to-sleep lullabies, but instead of the usual words, she sang "La, la, la," all the way through. She looked right into Howie's eyes and opened her mouth carefully as if she were trying to teach him to say "l."

I watched the way she opened her lips and moved her tongue up and down. I noticed that it stopped just behind her top teeth while she began the "l" sound.

As soon as we stopped, I led Howie away from the wagons to find a private place to practice. I tried and tried, again and again, to say "l." Finally I had it. I felt like I'd been climbing a long way up a mountain before I got to the top. I wanted to shout "I did it!" and listen for the echo to come back—*I did it. . . .*

Instead, I just grinned to myself, took Howie's hand, and led him back to the camp.

Mama was busy stirring gravy over the campfire. I handed the baby to Caroline, tiptoed quietly in back of Mama, and hugged her from behind. The nubby wool of her sweater felt rough against my cheek, and she turned, with a smile, to see who it was. Quickly, before my courage could fail me, I blurted out, "I love Mama."

She dropped the spoon, spun around, grabbed me in her arms, and hugged me so hard I could hardly breathe. "Oh, Dora," she whispered with a sob in her voice. "You *can* talk. You can! Bless you, child."

Tears were shining in her eyes when she let me go and said, "You've been planning that surprise for quite a while, haven't you?"

I nodded.

"Let's go find Papa right now and tell him," she said.

I shook my head, put my finger to my lips, and said *Shhh.*

"Oh," she said, "I understand. You want to surprise him yourself."

I nodded and ran to look for him. He was hobbling the horses for the night so they couldn't wander away and get lost. When I got close enough, I called, "Pa–pa, Pa–pa," and he looked up, laughed out loud, and opened his arms for me to run into.

"Say that again," he whispered as he squeezed me tight.

"Papa, Papa."

"Hallelujah! Hosanna! And hip-hip-hooray!!!" he shouted. "My darling Dora can talk at last. Finally I'm going to find out some of the things you've been waiting so long to tell me." He ruffled my hair fondly.

"Does Mama know?"

I nodded.

"Ed and Caroline?" he asked.

"No," I said.

"Then let's go tell them," he said and tugged me toward camp without noticing that I was shaking my head.

"Oh, come on," he coaxed, when I pulled back. "They've been waiting patiently and they deserve to know."

I had to agree he had a point.

When Caroline learned I could talk, she jumped to such a quick conclusion that I wished she'd never found out.

We no sooner had sat down to eat supper than she said, "Now

Dora can talk, she should take her turn at saying the blessing on the food."

"No!" I gasped, panicked by the idea.

"I believe who says the prayer is my decision," Papa reminded her.

"Oh, I wasn't deciding," Caroline said, "just suggesting."

"Don't be in such a hurry, Caroline," Mama said sternly. "Dora will decide when and where she wants to talk. And we'll give her as much time as she needs." She looked around the table, stopping briefly at each face. "Do all of you understand?"

After everyone agreed with a nod or a *yes*, Papa said the blessing himself.

"I love Mama," I whispered in her ear.

That evening, after Papa wrote *October 18* on his map, he added, *Dora speaks!!!!!!*

I made my sixteenth watermelon wedge different from all the others by embroidering ten black seeds on the pink part, the same number as the words I'd said.

Even the scenery became exciting at that part of the trip. Colorful rocks appeared on both sides of the road. They seemed to grow taller and taller and brighter and brighter until we were surrounded by all kinds of wonderful, red-rock formations.

It looked like some giant had carved a batch of brightly-colored soap into all sorts of in-and-out, roundabout patterns with his pocketknife. The leftover scraps were still scattered all over the ground. I drew a few of the fantastic rocky formations in my notebook. Some looked like cathedrals or pipe organs, others like groups of people. As we rode along, there were peaks and pinnacles, arches and balancing rocks as far as we could see.

"It looks like fireworks exploding to celebrate," Papa told me.

"Cel–e–bwa–ting what?" I asked.

"That you can talk," he said.

So that is how I remember the red-rock country just before we camped at Moab.

The scenery celebration lasted most of the way to Monticello, the last town we'd come to in Utah.

A wagon train the size of ours passing through was a rare event in this isolated community. Men, women, and children came out of their houses to greet us.

As in most Utah towns, almost all the people were members of the Latter-day Saint Church. They were excited that we shared the same religion, and each traveling family was invited to stay with a local one.

"We won't find this kind of hospitality again," Papa said, "so enjoy it as much as you can. Tomorrow we'll say good-bye to Utah. Maybe forever."

"Oh, Albert, don't say that," Mama objected with a catch in her voice. "Not forever."

"Well, for a long time at least," he said. "We'd better load up with water and anything else we might need. The next stretch, across the corner of Colorado, is going to be hot, dry, and desolate."

Papa didn't mention the other thing he expected in that corner of Colorado.

CHAPTER EIGHT

IN INDIAN COUNTRY

The first clue to what might be ahead came the next morning when the men were busy packing up and planning the day. I pricked up my ears when I heard Brother Coldwell ask, "Could that be a problem?"

Could what be a problem?

"Depends on which tribe," Papa said.

Tribe? Did he mean Indians? My skin popped out in goose bumps and my heart banged double time in my chest. Didn't Indians scalp people?

"Navajos won't be any trouble," Papa continued. "Utes might like to scare us. Both have reservations close to Cortez, the town we're heading for."

"What could we do?" Brother Lenstrom asked.

"Act friendly," Papa suggested.

"Keep smiling," Brother Coldwell added.

"Would it help if I played a cheery tune on my fiddle?" Brother Lenstrom asked.

"Probably would. . . ." Papa agreed. " . . . And . . . "

I could tell by the way he left the last word hanging in the air that he was figuring out something in his head.

Finally Papa said, "I know what we can do," but I didn't find out what it was, because he began to speak like he was telling a secret. The three men crouched down while he sketched something in the dirt. After a while they all got up and went back to their wagons.

Even though it wasn't wash day, Papa put water in the wash barrel. When others saw him do it, they filled their barrels, too.

"Our wagon will lead today," Papa announced as he harnessed up the horses.

"How come?" Mama wanted to know.

"Just because," Papa told her.

"Just because why?" Mama persisted.

"*Just because*," Papa said firmly in his I-can't-tell-you-that-right-now voice. I knew he didn't want to get her upset by mentioning Indians.

"What about taking some ice?" Mama asked coolly, to change the subject.

"There's an icehouse just out of town," Papa replied. "We'll get some."

Just before we left, Papa unfastened most of the reeds he'd gathered and dropped them in the wash barrel.

"What fo'?" I asked. I still couldn't say "r."

"Just in case I need them," he said.

Could the reeds have anything to do with Papa's plan?

We stopped at the icehouse and bought as big a piece as we could carry in the dishpan. Later, we were plenty glad we had it.

Ed and I rode next to Papa on the driver's seat. All we could see for miles and miles in every direction was desert. There was not a tree in sight, only sagebrush, rabbit brush, and dried-up grass. The October sun was hot. Heat waves curled up in ghostly spirals. Reflected sunlight shimmered and danced across the wide wasteland. Clouds of choking dust followed the wagons and the drivers behind us slowed a little to let it settle.

After a while Papa stopped the wagon to give the horses a drink.

"They're doing all the work in this heat," he said. "They need plenty of water. You do, too," he told us, and brought out tin cups filled with ice chips for Ed and me.

By then, the Coldwells' and Lenstroms' wagons had stopped behind ours. The three men had a short conversation, then Papa climbed back onto the seat and clucked to the horses to start up again.

"Look, Papa," Ed said. "There's a pond up there. We could have waited to water the horses."

"A pond?" Papa sounded surprised. "In the desert?"

"Yes. See that water up there?"

I could see it, too, and pointed to show Papa.

"See, Papa?" I said.

"Oh, yes," he replied, "it does look like a pond, doesn't it?"

"Yeah," Ed agreed. "Can we stop and wade in it to cool off our feet?"

"I wish we could," Papa said. "It would feel so good. But that's not really water. It's only a mirage."

"What's a mirage?" Ed asked.

"A mean trick of the desert," Papa explained. "The hot air causes a reflection of the sky and it looks like water shimmering in the sand. Lots of travelers have been fooled by it. Many have died of thirst thinking they would soon be to water."

I was glad we had water in the barrels and some ice, even if it was melting fast.

A few minutes later Ed pointed ahead. "Look," he said, "there's a people mirage."

"A what?" Papa asked.

"A people mirage. Looks like two somebodies up there shimmering in the sand."

Maybe ideas flew in and out of Ed's head like feathers on the breeze, but there was certainly nothing wrong with his eyesight. I could barely see two dark spots far in the distance. Could it be . . . ?

I continued to watch. The shapes didn't fade or keep moving ahead of us like the mirage did. They became larger and seemed to multiply as we got closer. First it looked like two people, then four, then more. They appeared to be on horses.

"Oh, oh," Papa said.

I grabbed his arm.

"Oh, oh, what?" Ed asked him.

"Looks like Indians," Papa said.

"Indians?" Ed gasped. He sounded scared, not excited.

"Stay calm and don't worry," Papa said. He guided the wagon

off the road and jumped down to the ground.

Just at that moment I heard a blood-curdling shriek. Cold shivers climbed up my backbone, and my heart started hammering so hard I could feel it in my ears. Ed's people mirage was not a trick of the desert but a *real* fast-moving cloud of dust and people racing toward us.

A half dozen bronze-colored riders on spotted horses pulled to a sudden stop. They scowled down at Papa, who was smiling as widely as he could.

"Friend," he greeted them and offered his hand. "Friend."

The Indians continued to stare wordlessly for a moment and then began shouting and waving their arms.

Papa shook his head as if he didn't understand and repeated the same word again, "Friend." He gestured toward the wagon and moved cautiously in that direction, followed by the Indians. Papa climbed up, reached down into the wash barrel and very slowly pulled out a handful of dripping reeds.

I decided that he didn't want to alarm the Indians by making any fast movements. They looked as puzzled as I felt. I couldn't believe what Papa did next.

He sat down on the ground and started to weave. It surely seemed like a silly time and place to make a basket.

Brother Coldwell's wagon pulled quietly close to ours. The Indians noticed. One growled something I couldn't understand.

Papa said nothing but kept on with his work, slowly lacing the reeds into a flat mat.

Brother Coldwell approached silently.

The Indian spoke again.

Papa nodded to acknowledge that he had heard, but stayed where he was. Nothing moved but his hands as he bent the ribs up and continued to weave until a basket began to take shape.

The angry expression on the Indian's face changed to curiosity. He slid off his pony and moved nearer, and the other riders followed his lead. Papa gestured at them to be seated, and they folded down in a cross-legged circle around him. Not a word was spoken.

Brother Lenstrom's wagon approached and moved next to Brother Coldwell's. I could see our usual nighttime circle starting to form.

Papa handed the basket to the nearest Indian, who wove one row around and then passed it to the next man in the circle.

A soft sigh came from Brother Lenstrom's fiddle. The music began so quietly that it blended with the whisper of the breeze through the desert grasses. The rhythm was the same as the in-and-out twining of the weavers. The basket went around and around the circle, Papa feeding in new strands as they were needed, Brother Lenstrom gradually increasing the tone and tempo of his song. The music seemed to flow into the blood of the weavers. Their bodies swayed back and forth, their hands moved like dancers.

The fourth wagon pulled into place, then the fifth.

When the weaving was six or seven inches from the top, Papa curved the pliable upright ribs into a looped border. He tucked in the ends and set the completed basket down in the center of the circle. Then he started another one, and while it went from man to man, he began one more. Then another, and another, until each Indian had his own.

When Papa stood up to get more materials, he signaled to Ed and me to climb down from the wagon. We slipped off the seat to the ground and watched quietly. Papa put some of the wet reeds in the center of the circle so the workers could help themselves, then stepped back and took my hand.

As the other wagons approached, one at a time, they stopped at their appointed places and the men climbed down cautiously to see what was going on. Other Indians appeared silently on foot and soon quite a crowd was watching the activity inside the protective circle that was closing around the weavers. I decided it must be part of Papa's plan to surround them.

I was afraid of what crazy thing Bradford and Benjamin Brownley might think up to spoil it. I turned to look behind me and caught sight of a large Indian woman coming toward me with a loop stretched open between her hands. She looked straight at me with a toothless grin. She moved closer and closer with that ring of rope in her hands. It was like a noose all ready to pop over my head to choke me. She grinned wider as she moved nearer and nearer. Her eyes were as dark as death.

Right while everyone was paying attention to making baskets that crazy woman was going to kill me! I tried to cry "Papa!" but my throat was paralyzed with fear, and no sound came out.

I buried my head under Papa's arm and squeezed him hard so he could tell that I was frightened. I felt him turn toward the woman to see what was happening. He laughed and lifted his arm off my face.

"It's all right, Dora," he assured me. "She won't hurt you. She brought you a present."

I peeked out to see what he was talking about, and the woman held out a beautiful string of dried berries and Indian beads. Her black eyes were dancing with pleasure. The toothless old smile was not wicked, after all, but warm.

She put the necklace she was carrying carefully over my head and stood back to admire the effect.

"Pretty," she said, "Pretty."

"She speaks English," Ed whispered to Papa and he nodded that he'd noticed.

"Some," he said.

The woman reached out cautiously to touch one of my yellow curls.

"Pretty," she said again. Her face beamed with happiness.

I climbed back in the wagon to get the mirror to see how the necklace looked.

As I lifted it from my wooden box, I remembered my string of beads. Suddenly, I wanted to give them to the Indian woman. I reached behind the Bible to pull them out.

When I slipped them over her head, I held the looking glass in front of her face.

"See?" I said, pointing to her image in the mirror.

I never saw anyone so happy.

"Pretty! Pretty!" she cried, laughing at her reflection.

I handed her the mirror to keep, too, and Papa reached out and squeezed my hand to show me I had done the right thing.

While the men worked and the others watched, Papa spoke to the woman in gentle tones. She could understand some English words but looked puzzled about others. When she did, Papa substituted some strange expressions I had never heard before.

He was talking about being friends and someone named Ralph Cookson. Must be a relative, I decided. The woman whispered the name to one of the men seated in the circle and he smiled and nodded.

Just then five more Indians came galloping up. The leader, who appeared to be the chief, had a small boy riding in front of him.

The weavers jumped up to show off their baskets and all the men began to speak rapidly in their own language.

Finally, after a lot of talking among the Indians, the chief spoke to Papa.

"Friend," he said and held out his hand. "Friend."

Papa shook it vigorously and repeated, "Friend."

He pulled out his pocketknife, opened and closed it to show how it worked, and handed it to the chief's son. The young boy tried it out and grinned his pleasure.

"We need to be on our way to find a camping place," Papa told the chief.

"Camp here," the chief said, pointing to the wagons already arranged in a circle.

Papa turned to Brother Coldwell for approval. He smiled and replied, "Why not? We all brought plenty of water today."

At the chief's signal, the Indians turned away and headed back. As soon as they were out of sight, Ed wiped his forehead and let out a big breath of air.

"Whew," he said. "That was a close call."

"Yup," Papa agreed.

"What kind of words were you speaking to the woman?"

"Navajo," Papa told him.

"How'd you learn that language?"

"My grandfather, Ralph Cookson, taught me to say a few things," Papa replied. "He did some negotiating with the Indians in pioneer times. I didn't know if we'd met up with Utes or Navajos. When the woman could understand me, I knew they were Navajos. I was glad, too. Utes are a more hostile tribe. When I mentioned Grandpa's name, she remembered him and so did some of the older Indians."

"They liked the baskets," Ed said.

"And the music," I added.

"Yup," Papa agreed.

"How'd you think of it?" Ed asked.

"Inspiration," Papa said, "pure inspiration. Navajos are wonderful weavers, but they only weave rugs. They don't make baskets. And the work is always done by the women. When the men saw me doing it, I guess that made it all right for them to try. And Brother Lenstrom's music sort of hypnotized them. Maybe they thought the whole thing was some kind of friendly white-man ceremony."

"Well, it sure worked," Ed said.

"Yup," Papa said, "it did."

CHAPTER NINE

A DELICATE CONDITION

Just before we left the campground the next morning, the Indian chief rode up. He had a gift for Papa—a large three-pronged stick shaped like a *Y*.

"That would make a powerful slingshot," Ed whispered to me.

The chief had a different idea.

"Find water," he said to Papa.

The chief held the stick by two of the branches with the third pointed straight ahead. He walked around, watching the end of it intently. All at once the branch tipped down until it pointed to the ground.

"Water there," the Indian said. "Dig well."

"I understand," Papa said. "It will find the right place to dig for water."

The chief nodded. He handed Papa the stick, jumped back on his horse, and rode away.

"What's that?" Mama asked, as Papa tucked the branch safely inside the wagon.

"A witching wand," he told her. "Sometimes it's called a divining rod."

"You mean one of those sticks that's supposed to find water?" Mama asked.

"Yup," Papa replied.

"That's just a silly superstition," Mama scoffed.

"Superstition or not," Papa said, "I'm going to keep it. It might come in handy."

Later that day, Sister Owens became ill, so we stopped early. She was a pretty lady with brown eyes—sort of plump, like Mama. Sister Lenstrom whispered that she was "in a delicate condition," and I took that to mean she must be kind of sickly.

In the middle of the night, I was wakened by moaning coming from a nearby wagon. Sister Owens must be in terrible pain. The noise kept up for a long time before someone scratched at our canvas wagon cover.

"Are you Doc Cookson?" Brother Owens asked Papa anxiously.

"Some people call me that," Papa replied with a laugh. "But I'm not a real medical-school doctor. What can I do for you?"

"The baby's coming early, and I don't know what to do. We expected to be in Clovis in plenty of time."

"Don't worry," Papa said soothingly. "I can help with that. I brought all six of ours into the world. One more won't be any trouble."

"I hope you can save the baby this time. We buried the last two."

A new baby was coming? How exciting! I started to wonder again how babies got down from heaven when it was time for them to be born. Did storks really carry them in little bundled-up packages? I was too small to remember about Ed and Frank, but George and Howie each had been wrapped up like that the first time I saw them.

Both times, all of us older children had been sleeping over at Grandma Cookson's house. As soon as we got home in the morning, Papa had said, "Mama has a surprise to show you. Go in the bedroom and see what it is."

Each time she was lying in bed holding the new baby, who was cuddled in a cozy blue blanket.

I couldn't figure out how Brother Owens knew when the baby was coming at all, much less how he could tell it would be early, and here instead of in Clovis. And why did he need a doctor? Just in case the stork dropped the bundle from heaven and the baby got hurt? Is that how the other two died? Was that what Sister Owens was making such a fuss about, because she was afraid of what might happen? And what could Papa do to help her? What did he mean when he said he'd brought all six of his own into the world?

There were lots of questions I needed to ask as soon as I could talk a little better. I wiggled out from under the wagon to see if I could spot a stork flying overhead. For what seemed like forever, I heard the groans in the Owens's wagon getting louder and closer together. I thought about the two babies left behind in the cemetery. Sister Owens must be worried something awful to be making so much noise about it. I hoped this baby would live. And I especially hoped it wouldn't be tongue-tied.

I didn't see a thing except stars, and I must have dozed off watching for the stork. All of a sudden I heard a new sound, a baby's cry, loud and angry, as if it were afraid of falling or else didn't want to leave heaven.

In the morning, Brother Coldwell announced that Brother and Sister Owens had a new daughter, Elizabeth Ann.

"We'll be leaving a couple of hours later than usual," he said.

Almost everyone in camp came by to see the new baby. She was wrapped in a pink blanket and seemed to be satisfied to be on Earth after all. She was beautiful. Sister Owens let me touch her angel-soft hair, and when she stuck out her tongue I knew it couldn't be tied down. Thank goodness for that! I heaved a big sigh of relief.

The darling baby girl made me wish for a little sister of my own. After four boys in a row, our family needed another girl. I wanted to make pretty clothes and dress her up like a doll. Girl or boy, though, when we had another baby in our family, the name would begin with I. Since Papa's initials were ABC, for Albert B. Cookson, and Mama's name, Betty, began with the second letter, they had decided to go on down the alphabet to name their children. So far we had Caroline, Dora, Ed, Frank, George, and Howie.

"Only eighteen more to go, hon," Papa teased Mama, "until we get to Z."

"I'll settle for an even dozen," she told Papa.

That meant six more babies. I counted that many letters on my fingers. We'd get to N.

I was still daydreaming about new babies when Ed found me.

"Come on, Dora," he said. "Let's get away from the wagons so we can be by ourselves."

Ever since I'd spoken my first words, Ed had been helping me learn to talk. I was surprised that someone who hated school knew as much as he did. He had started with "a" and proceeded through the alphabet, teaching me how to make the sounds of all the letters. We were working on "g".

"Sometimes 'g' sounds like the beginning of George," he said, "and sometimes it sounds like the end of dog."

"Or G-G-GRR, as in G-G-GRIZZLY bear!" a deeper voice growled.

I jumped at the sudden sound.

"GRIZZLY bear!" came an echo.

The Brownley boys had followed us.

"When's Dumb Dora gonna learn to talk?" Bradford wanted to know.

"Yeah, when?" Benjamin asked.

"She's learning," Ed insisted.

"I thought you said she had her tongue fixed," Bradford went on.

"Yeah, that's what you said." Benjamin chimed in.

"She did," Ed agreed.

"Didn't help much, did it?" Bradford said.

"No, it didn't, did it?" Benjamin repeated.

"Takes a long time to learn to talk," Ed told them.

"Well, are you the only one who can teach her?" Bradford asked.

"Yeah, the only one?" Benjamin echoed.

"Why can't Caroline do it?" Bradford suggested.

"Yeah, let Caroline do it," Benjamin agreed.

"Then you could do some real boys' things without that pesky sister tagging along."

"Yeah, she's a regular tag-along," Benjamin said.

"Why don't you tell her to beat it?" Bradford suggested.

"Beat it!" echoed Benjamin, looking straight at me.

By that time, I was so mad I wanted those Brownley boys to beat it. Forever. I wished the earth would open up and swallow them. I wanted to sprout wings and fly back to Utah and get Ilene. Her exclamation-point fist would set those bratty brothers straight in a hurry. She'd let them know that even a girl who can't talk very well has feelings, the same as anyone else.

Like most of the boys in camp, Ed was scared of the Brownleys. He did whatever they insisted on. When Bradford said, "We're going to play Kick the Can," Ed got the can. If Brad decided on Pop the Whip, he put Ed at the end so he flew off first.

Today they wanted some horny toads. The Brownleys were too slow and clumsy to catch the spiny, skittish creatures, but they wanted some to tease the girls. They loved to drop the ugly lizards in our hair, put them down our backs, or toss them in our food.

They knew Ed was the best horny toad catcher in the camp. He could sneak up quietly and grab them quickly before they got away. He was proud of his ability, too. That's probably why he went with Brad and Benjie.

I hated those troublemaking brothers. Would they quit teasing me when I could talk properly? Would I ever learn how?

I remembered how happy I'd been when the doctor said he would fix my tongue. How long ago was that? It seemed like a lifetime. Some sounds were still impossible to say. I sighed and returned to the wagon to count the watermelon scallops on my sampler. There were twenty-three.

After a while, Ed came back.

"Catch any?" I asked.

"Two," he said. "One for Bradford, one for Benjamin. They wanted more, but I told them that was enough.'"

"Good," I said.

"I told them that I'm sick and tired of being their slave."

"You did?"

"Yup," he replied.

"How did you get bwave enough?"

As soon as the words were out, my mouth dropped open in astonishment. Had I really said that whole sentence? I couldn't believe it. Except for one "r", the pronunciation was perfect. I grinned my pleasure while Ed answered the question.

"I just did," he said.

"What did they say?" I asked, continuing the conversation with another sentence.

"Bradford made a mean face and said 'OH? Is that so?'" Ed imitated Brad's scowl.

"And?" I pursued.

"And Benjamin said, 'OH? Is that so?' just as sassy as you please."

"Sounds like twouble," I predicted.

"Yeah, I know," Ed replied. "They didn't like it. They'll think of something mean to do to get even."

"Yes, they will," I agreed.

CHAPTER TEN

PAGOSA SPRINGS

Ed and I were worried that the Brownley boys would play an unpleasant trick on him the next day, but nothing bad happened for a long time. By the time it did, we'd almost forgotten we were fearful.

We left the dry, treeless desert behind and gradually began the climb into the San Juan mountains. We traveled up and down hills and across high plateaus. There were more streams, more trees, and more feed for the cows and horses. More food for us, too. The scouts who rode ahead often caught fish or killed game for supper.

We had deer, elk, wild turkeys, and grouse.

"This is the highest any of us have ever been," Papa said as we pulled into our campground. "The elevation is nearly eight thousand feet. Has anyone noticed it's harder to breathe up here?"

No wonder I huffed and puffed so much when we all had to walk to help the horses up the hills. No wonder they needed us to lighten the load.

When Papa flipped the calendar to November, we weren't much more than halfway to Clovis. The nights were cool enough for frost. I wasn't surprised to see clouds of smoke from evening fires billowing into the sky as we approached the town of Pagosa Springs.

As we got closer, however, a peculiar smell, not smoky, was in the air. Papa sniffed.

"Must be sulfur springs here," he said. "I wonder if Pagosa is an Indian word for sulfur. Or maybe hot. They sure are steaming."

"Hot springs?" Mama exclaimed. "Oh, Albert, do you think we might . . . ?"

Mama loved to soak in the hot mineral baths just north of Salt Lake City back in Utah.

"Wouldn't be surprised," Papa answered. "You probably aren't the only one who would like a nice hot bath."

"I would!" I said.

Where we stopped to camp, small springs were bubbling out of the ground in several places, right next to a slow-moving stream.

"Well now," Papa said as we pulled off to camp, "isn't that handy? If the springwater is too hot, you can cool it with the river water. No matter what temperature you want, you can have it."

When we woke up the next morning, the whole world looked like a fairyland. The warm mist from the springs had frozen into hoarfrost. Each stalk and stem, every bush and seed and berry wore a coat of ice that looked like spun crystal. The dried weed patches were tiny fairy forests covered with snow, just the right size for elves, pixies, and sprites.

Papa and some of the other men rode into town from our camping place to find out where we could swim. They located the Great Hot Springs, a public bathhouse.

"Pagosa Springs is a booming metropolis," Papa told us when he got back. "It has three grocery stores, three meat markets, two hardware stores, a bank, a bakery, a wagon and carriage shop, and even a gent's furnishings store. And a flour mill. How's our flour supply?" he asked Mama.

"Getting low," she replied.

"We'll buy a bag," he promised. "I found out that *Pagosa* is an Indian name meaning 'healing waters.' Everyone who bathes today should be healthy for a while."

"That'll be a blessing," Mama said.

Right after breakfast, Bradford and Benjamin came by to get Ed.

"Come on, Ed," Bradford announced. "We're goin' fishin'."

"Yeah, fishin'," Benjie echoed.

"Without yer pesky sister who can't even talk yet," Bradford insisted.

"Yeah," Benjie agreed, staring straight at me. "Leave Dumb Dora here."

I thought about Ilene and her powerful punch, how she'd fix those mean boys in a hurry if she were here. Clearly, I'd have to stand up to them someday. But how? I'd never go after them with my fists. Fighting wasn't the way the Cooksons solved problems.

"Thought I'd go swimmin' with everybody else," Ed replied to Bradford's demand.

"*Swimmin*'?" Bradford exploded. "You don't mean sissy swimmin'? In that *warm* water?"

"Not sissy swimmin'," Benjie repeated.

"You wanna go swimmin', we'll swim in the river," Bradford said.

"Yeah, the river," Benjie agreed.

"I don't want . . . " Ed began. He hated cold water.

"He *don't want*," Bradford shouted. "Did you get that, Benjie?"

"Got it," Benjie said, "he don't want . . ."

"We'll teach him to *don't want*," Bradford announced.

"Yeah," Benjie agreed, "we'll teach him."

The boys moved closer to Ed, grabbed him under the elbows and carried him away. They disappeared around a bend downstream, and soon I heard a big splash, followed by Ed's loud scream of protest.

He was soaked to the skin and shivering when he came back by himself.

"I'm n-n-never going to play with those b-b-ig b-bullies again," he said, his teeth chattering.

I wondered how he'd avoid them.

"It's a good thing the Great Hot Springs are here to thaw you out," Papa said. "Take off those cold clothes and we'll go swimming."

After Ed finally got warmed up in the pool, he wanted to go fishing.

"Come on, Dora," he said, as he untied his willow pole and

pulled out the shovel for digging worms. I found an empty tin can to put the wriggly bait in.

We hadn't seen the Brownley boys since they'd dumped Ed in the river. Just to be sure we didn't meet them, we went in the opposite direction—up the stream. We didn't go far. Being out of earshot was against camp rules.

When we were alone, I tried talking some more.

"Look at that frog!" Ed shouted. He dropped the things he was carrying and bounded across the mossy stones to grab it.

"Fwog," I said. "Fwog."

"Not fwog," Ed corrected. "Frog . . . frrrr . . . Lift up your tongue, like this." He showed me what he meant.

I tried it. "Fwrrrog," I said.

"That's better," he encouraged. "Now keep practicing." He examined the frog. "What a beauty," he marveled. "Look how big it is. I wonder how far it can jump."

"Let's twy it," I suggested.

"Try," Ed said, "trrry. Lift up your tongue!"

I guess the lift-up muscles in my tongue hadn't been used enough to know what to do. Most of the sounds I couldn't say seemed to be made with the end of my tongue in the top of my mouth.

To measure how far the frog could jump, Ed placed it on a starting line he'd marked with the fishing pole. Then I touched the frog's back with a stick to make it jump. I walked ahead to mark the place where it landed and Ed measured the distance with his feet. We stayed until nearly dark, following the frog as it leaped along, counting how many footsteps for each jump. We never did go fishing. Neither of us noticed how late it was getting until we heard Papa calling. Ed picked up the frog, and we ran to meet him.

"Look at my frog, Papa," Ed said.

"That's a fine one, all right," Papa agreed.

"Can I keep it?" Ed asked. "Can I?"

"No, son," Papa said. "You'd better leave it here."

"But I need a pet," Ed argued.

Papa shook his head. "It would only die if you took it."

"No it wouldn't," Ed insisted. "I'll put it in a bucket of water. And feed it. And . . ."

"A bucket of water isn't the same as a stream. This is where it belongs."

"Please, Papa."

"No, Ed. Now put it down, and I'll tell you a story on the way back." Papa reached for my hand.

"What about?" Ed asked.

"About a frog."

"A true story?"

"Would I tell any other kind?"

True or not, Papa's stories were always worth listening to.

Ed put his pet in a protected spot by the stream. He picked up the can of worms and the fishing pole and reached for Papa's other hand. The three of us began to walk toward camp.

"What's the story?" Ed wanted to know.

"How butter was discovered."

"You said it was about a frog."

"So it is. You see, a long time ago a frog jumped into a bowl of cream that was left by a dairy maid to keep cool at the edge of a stream. The maid's name was Betty."

"Mama?" I asked.

"No," Papa replied, "a different Betty. The frog paddled around all night trying to get out, and when Betty came the next morning to get the cream, she found a lump of butter swimming in some watery buttermilk."

"Was the frog still in it?"

"Probably," Papa said, "but Betty sure didn't tell anyone. Since there was no cream to spread, she used the butter instead. She sprinkled it, as usual, with a dash of salt and a spoonful of sugar. Everyone liked the new spread, even better than cream. When the first batch was gone, her mistress asked her to make more."

"Did she figure out the frog had done it?" Ed asked.

"I guess so," Papa said. "Anyway, she stirred and stirred and stirred some cream until it turned out the same as the day before. They called it 'Betty's better spread' until someone changed the name to 'Betty's butter.'"

"Oh, Papa," Ed said. "You just made up that story."

"Me? Make up a story?" Papa seemed surprised that anyone could think such a thing. "I'd never do that, would I?"

We couldn't tell if he would or not.

By then, we were back at the campground, smelling the rainbow trout Mama had sizzling in the frying pan. After supper, the babies were put to bed inside the wagons and the rest of us sat around the fire. Soon Brother Lenstrom's fiddle began its tune, and the grown-ups were moving their feet to the music. While we watched the dancing, I tried out the "frr" sound with my tongue.

"F-f-fr-fr-frrog. Frog," I whispered to Ed.

"That's good, Dora," he said. "Very good."

The next morning, the women decided to fill the wash barrels while we were close to such nice hot water. They tossed in the dirty clothes and added some homemade lye soap. The jogging of the wagons would slosh the laundry clean while we rode along. We'd camp earlier than usual so the women could rinse the wash in a stream while the men strung clotheslines between the trees.

"They'll need more rinsing than usual today," Mama said, "to get rid of the sulfur smell."

Wash day was always a busy time, and all of us had to help out more than usual. While Papa finished filling the barrel with steaming water, Mama assigned the chores we each needed to take care of after we stopped.

"Caroline, you and Frank take care of the chickens," she instructed. "Make sure they are fed and watered and don't let any of them get lost when you turn them out to run. Don't spend so much time petting that rooster that you forget the hens."

"Dora, I'll need you to watch George and Howie while I rinse and hang the clothes. Ed, you can churn the butter."

"I hate to churn butter," Ed objected. "Let Caroline do it."

"She has her own jobs," Mama told him.

"Butter churning is girls' work," he insisted.

"Don't argue with me, young man," Mama said in her I-won't-put-up-with-any-nonsense voice. "Half an hour's work isn't worth making such a fuss about. You can do it while we ride along if you want to," she said, encouragingly. "Then it will be done by the time we stop. We need it for supper."

Just then I saw the look come into Ed's eyes that meant he had an idea. I knew what it was because I had it, too.

CHAPTER ELEVEN

CHURNING THE BUTTER

Without wasting any time, Ed jerked his head at me in a way that said, "Come on." He grabbed a bar of soap and a towel, and we ran off in the direction of the stream.

"Where are you two going?" Mama called, and Ed shouted, "To wash our hands."

"You lied," I reminded him when we stopped by the creek.

"No I didn't," he replied, "we'll wash our hands."

The frog was still where we had left it the night before. Being cold-blooded, it had to warm up before it would move much.

Ed picked up the frog and started to lather it with the soap. I gave him my "What are you doing?" look.

"Getting it clean enough." Ed rinsed the soap off in the stream, patted the frog dry, and tucked it inside his shirt.

We scrubbed our hands to make us honest and stayed by the stream, cutting some willows to take with us. It's a good thing we did, because we found the shovel Ed had dropped the day before when he first caught the frog. At the last minute, we ran to the wagon and jumped in the back.

Mama sat in front with Papa, holding George on her lap. Frank and Caroline were each walking with a friend, and Howie was asleep. We had the whole place to ourselves.

Ed plopped the frog into the butter churn, and we settled down for a lazy ride. It's lucky we had the kind of churn we did. One like the Lenstroms', with a paddle wheel turned by a handle wouldn't work. It had too many jumping-out-to-rest places where a frog could sit without even being in the cream. Ours didn't have a dasher or a paddle. It was like a small keg turned on its side. The handle rocked it back and forth like a cradle, and the movement sloshed the cream into butter. The frog had to swim.

We reached over the tailgate, dragging our willows in the dust to make patterned trails behind us. After a while, Ed decided to show me how to make willow whistles. But the bark cracked and wouldn't slip off the way it was supposed to.

"Wrong time of year, I guess," he said. "Sap's all dried up."

Several times we peeked into the churn, where the frog was still swimming around. There was no sign of butter. Ed started trying to teach me to say "Betty's better spread," and we forgot about everything else until the wagon stopped for our noon meal.

As soon as we climbed out, Mama asked, "Did the butter come yet?"

"Not yet," Ed told her.

"Have you been working at it, or just daydreaming?" Mama asked.

"Yeah," Ed said, without answering which.

"Well you'd better get it done before supper," she said sternly, "or else you'll be in trouble."

Papa told her the frog story, and she said, "Now Albert, don't go giving those children any crazy ideas. It would be just like Ed and Dora to try that out.

"*And don't you dare!*" she warned, shaking her finger at us.

Ed and I both expected Mama to check in the churn that very minute to see if we were already guilty. Luckily, she was too busy. We didn't dare look at each other for fear she would notice and get even more suspicious. We stayed close to the wagon, however, watching and waiting anxiously for a chance to get that frog out of the cream before she found it.

When we finished eating, we jumped quickly back into the wagon, and Ed heaved a big sigh of relief as if he'd been holding his breath for a very long time. "That was close," he whispered. I nodded.

Just then Caroline climbed in, followed by Frank. They had both decided they wanted to ride in the wagon now. They settled down right next to the churn.

I stared at Ed with my what-do-we-do-now look, and he shrugged his I-don't-know answer.

I knew he didn't want to start rocking the churn as fast as we usually did for fear he'd bang the frog against the sides and kill it—maybe even mash it to a pulp. But we both knew he had to have some butter in time for supper.

"You'd better start churning," Caroline reminded Ed in a bossy voice.

"I will," he said, but he didn't move a muscle to do it.

"I'm gonna tell Mama," Caroline threatened.

Ed reached for the handle and moved it back and forth very slowly.

"You'll never get butter that way," Caroline told him.

"Mind your own business!" Ed exploded. "You do your work and I'll do mine."

"Well, don't say I didn't warn you," Caroline shot back. "See if I care if you get a licking." She tossed her head, opened the book she'd borrowed from Sarah Lenstrom, and began to read.

Frank soon fell asleep, and Ed leaned back, yawned loudly and closed his eyes. I could tell from the way he looked at me and then at Caroline that he was hoping to make her sleepy, too, and that I was supposed to wake him up if she dozed off. No such luck. Caroline was as wide awake as her pet rooster at daybreak.

I could feel my own eyes getting heavy, but I knew I had to watch for a chance to take care of that frog. I fought to stay awake. I decided to work on the sampler and took it carefully from the chest. I counted the finished melon slices. Thirty-three. Eleven more to go and the border would be finished. Would we be in Clovis by then? Would I be able to go to school in New Mexico? I hoped so.

The sampler could tell about that. I'd put a crooked, slammed door in the top left corner. Down at the bottom, like a happily-ever-after story, would be an open door—a nice, clean, painted-white door. The one to the schoolhouse. In between the two doors, I could make pictures of the things that happened on the trip from Utah to New Mexico. Jumping rope . . . red-rock fireworks . . . Indians weaving baskets . . . Pagosa Spr . . .

The next thing I knew, Papa was calling "Whoa!" to the horses and the wagon slowed down to a stop. Ed was asleep, the frog was still in the churn, and I couldn't tell if the cream had been kicked into butter or not.

The sun was still high in the sky. I remembered it was wash day and we were stopping early to rinse and dry the clothes. Frank and Ed woke up, and I helped Frank climb down over the tailgate.

Caroline put a marker in her book and slammed it shut. She stepped past Ed and me and said, "I'm going to tell Mama you didn't make the butter."

Ed stuck his tongue out at her. He grabbed the churn handle and yelled, "I'm doing it now."

As soon as she was out of sight, he lifted the lid to rescue the frog. It sat high on top of an island of butter. A green frog with black spots on creamy butter, a perfect picture for my sampler.

"Butter," I said. "Frog."

I had finally said "r." Twice. Ed noticed.

"Good for you, Dora!" he said as he grabbed the frog and tucked it inside his shirt in one quick movement. He closed the lid of the churn and jumped down from the wagon with me right behind him.

"Butter's done," he called to Mama.

"Good boy!" she called back. "I knew you could do it."

"I don't believe it," Caroline said and looked to see. "It must have churned itself," she muttered. "Ed didn't do it."

He took off for the stream as fast as he could go to turn the frog loose and I followed, with George holding one hand and Howie the other.

Neither Ed nor I ever told how the butter was churned that day. No matter how pretty a picture, I couldn't give our secret away by putting it on the sampler.

Papa didn't tell, either. But I knew he knew. Every time he reached for the butter dish, he winked at me.

The Brownley boys came by for Ed, just as if nothing had happened the day before. They had a smelly collection to brag about.

"Boiled frogs," Bradford said, pulling a pie plate from behind him. It was piled high with dead frogs.

"Yeah," Benjie repeated, "boiled."

"That's what we found when we went fishin'," Bradford explained, "in the boiling hot bug holes by the river. They just jumped in and cooked themselves."

"Jumped and cooked," Benjie repeated.

I could tell by the way Ed looked at me that he was glad we'd saved one frog from jumping into a hot spring.

I wondered how he planned to save himself from the Brownleys.

CHAPTER TWELVE

LEAVING CIVILIZATION

Today we leave Colorado and enter New Mexico," Papa announced the next day at breakfast. "We'll be going from a state to a territory."

"You mean New Mexico isn't even a state?" Mama asked.

"Nope," Papa said. "Not yet. It belongs to the United States, but it's not a state."

"Oh, dear." Mama sounded worried. "We're leaving civilization to live in the wilderness."

Papa laughed. "No we're not. You'd never know the difference if I hadn't told you."

"Are we nearly to the homestead?" Ed asked.

"Not yet," Papa said, spreading out the map and pointing to the end of his marked line. "We're right here on the Colorado border."

Below Colorado, a big space was boxed in by the same kind of edge. It looked like a state to me.

Papa's finger followed a diagonal route that cut deep across the upper right hand corner. "Clovis is down here near the edge of Texas," he said.

"Oh my." Mama sighed. "It's a long way yet."

"Yep," Papa agreed. "We'd better get going."

We traveled gradually downhill along the river, making as much distance each day as we could. Trees grew farther and farther apart, except along the stream, where golden cottonwoods gleamed in the autumn sunlight.

Papa was wrong when he said we wouldn't notice the difference in New Mexico. When we came to the bustling city of Santa Fe, I felt like we were in a foreign country for sure. All the buildings had a strange, round-cornered look. Papa said they were made of adobe clay instead of boards. Most of the people had brown skin, black eyes, and dark hair. The girls wore brightly colored clothes and lots of silver jewelry set with turquoise stones. They didn't even speak English.

"Looks like lots of Mexicans live here," Mama observed.

"Yup," Papa agreed. "Mexicans settled this part of the country. That's why it's called *New* Mexico."

"Lots of Indians, too," Mama said.

"That's right," Papa said. "They make the jewelry."

The Lenstrom wagon pulled to the side of the road ahead of us in front of a store. Papa stopped behind it.

"While we're in town," he said, "I want to get another pocket-knife."

"We need a bag of cornmeal, too," Mama said.

"Pink and green thread," I added.

"Bring your lists," Papa told us.

After we made our purchases, we hurried on our way again.

Mama's worry that we'd be leaving civilization and heading for the wilderness seemed to come true soon after we left Santa Fe. The hills gradually gave way to flat land and all the trees disappeared. Before long, we spotted spiny cacti scattered among the sparse brushy growth. Mile after mile, day after dreary day, we traveled through desert wasteland.

Papa's predicted travel time of five or six weeks was all used up, and we were nowhere near Clovis. I finished the scalloped border around my sampler—forty-four watermelon smiles. I drew more slices in my notebook to keep track of the number of days, but I made them upside down, like frowns.

We saw no houses, no people. No horses. No cows or chickens except those in our wagon train. Lizards, horny toads, and rattlesnakes seemed to be the only animals that lived in New Mexico.

Supplies were getting low. Fresh meat was impossible to find. We ate the chickens one by one.

"I'm glad you thought to bring them," Papa told Mama. "We're all thankful for your foresight."

Back in Utah, when Papa was so excited about the chance to have a place of our own, I'd expected we'd find beautiful green farms with miles and miles of watermelon patches in New

Mexico. Where were they? Even in November there should be some withered vines and rotting fruit left in the fields. But there weren't any fields. There was only dry, sandy desert with ugly, prickly cacti.

I was tired of the desert, tired of the trip, even tired of trying to talk. Once I learned to pronounce "r," I was able to string words together in sentences. I had plenty of things I wanted to say. But my mind could think of ideas much faster than my mouth could say them.

Then another problem arose: I stuttered. My lips often trembled on the easy beginning sounds of a word while I concentrated on forming the difficult parts that followed. The more nervous I became, the worse it was. I hated it.

"Don't worry," Mama said encouragingly. "You'll soon learn how to stop stuttering."

How was I supposed to learn? Howie couldn't show me. Ed didn't know. Talking was so difficult. No matter how hard I tried, some new problem always came up to stop me. What would be next? I didn't want to know.

The Brownley brothers must have been sorry about dumping Ed in the creek, because they'd been nice to him ever since Pagosa Springs. The three of them spent a lot of time hunting horny toads.

"Might as well," Ed said. "There's nothing else to do."

One day Bradford killed a rattlesnake. He'd been shaking the rattlers ever since to beat time to his teasing.

"D-D-D-Dora," (rattle, rattle) "what a b-bore-a," (rattle, rattle) he sang.

Benjie echoed, "D-dora, the b-big b-bore-a."

I hated those brats. But at least I could stick my tongue out at them now. It didn't bother them much but I enjoyed doing it.

Sarah Lenstrom and Caroline spent a lot of time together, so Jenny and I did, too. Jenny had a beautiful shut-eye doll named Samantha, who had lots of clothes. I took Henrietta and her things out of my chest, and we played house together, using Jenny's set of china dishes for pretend tea parties. Time went faster when I spent it with Jenny.

Caroline and Sarah organized a jacks tournament to see who was the best player in the company. For a while, that kept most of us girls busy every evening. The only flat surface we could find to play on was Sister Lenstrom's bread board. We all wore our fingernails down to the quick trying to pick up the jacks. Caroline and Sarah tied for the championship. They were happy to share the title and decided not to play another game to break the tie.

"From now on, we'll just play for fun," Caroline announced.

Each night when Papa traced the short line on the map indicating how far we'd traveled, he pointed to Clovis, marked with a star. It still seemed as far away as the stars in the sky.

Finally, on the forty-ninth day after leaving Holladay, we came to Fort Sumner, where Brother Talbot was in charge of the land office.

"This place may not look like much," Papa said, "but it's very important."

"For what?" I wanted to know.

"It's where we sign up for our homestead."

We arrived on a Sunday night and camped outside of town. Early the next morning we pulled our line of wagons in front of the U.S. government building.

Brother Talbot came outside to welcome us and introduced himself to each family in turn.

"I thought you'd never get here," he said to Papa.

"We wondered, too," Papa told him.

"Let's see." Brother Talbot consulted his list. "Albert Cookson. Yes. The papers are all ready for you to sign. Your place is past Clovis. Almost to Texico, in fact."

"Texico?" Papa asked.

"That's right," Brother Talbot said. "Half the town's in Texas, half's in New Mexico. The state line runs right through the middle. So does the railroad. Brother and Sister Williamson live near there. They'll show you where your piece is."

"How do I find them?" Papa asked.

Brother Talbot laughed. "Ask anyone within ten miles," he said. "By the way, Mr. Hoyt hasn't moved his family out of the homestead house yet, so he's found a temporary place for you to stay."

"That's fine," Papa said. "How much farther is it?"

"About sixty miles to Clovis," Brother Talbot said. "Ten more to Texico."

"Seventy miles!" Mama exclaimed. "That'll take four more days."

"Not quite," Mr. Talbot said. "You'll have to hurry to get there in time for Thanksgiving dinner with the Williamsons. They're expecting you."

Thanksgiving dinner? No one had mentioned that this was the week of Thanksgiving. I had almost forgotten what it was like to be invited to sit down and have a bite to eat. But I remembered in a hurry and started getting hungry.

"That's an appropriate day to arrive," Papa said. "We'll have plenty to be thankful for."

Brother Talbot handed Papa a map. "Your piece is outlined in red," he said, pointing with a pencil. "And the Williamsons live here." Mr. Talbot made an X not far from the red square.

"Where's the school?" Mama wanted to know.

"Half a mile west of your place," Brother Talbot said. He wrote an S to show her.

"And the church?"

"In Clovis. Right about here." Brother Talbot made a C on the map. "It's a big house on the corner," he added.

We set out with great eagerness on the final leg of the journey to our new home. The last few days seemed like the longest part of the trip. Why did it take everyone so long to get going in the morning? Why did the horses move so slowly and stop so often to eat? Why did it get dark before we had a chance to travel very far?

I had never seen such flat land. Not a sign of a rise anywhere. The ground was reddish brown, not black like the dirt I was used to in our Utah garden. It looked like Mother Nature had spread a big batch of gingerbread dough with a giant rolling pin, sprinkled it with cinnamon and left it in the sun to bake. Dust devils rose up like puffs of powdered spice, and I could almost smell the tempting fragrance.

When we finally neared Clovis, the wagons pulled off, one by one, in different directions. I was glad to see the Brownleys go first. That meant their homestead would be the farthest away from ours.

"'Bye," Ed called as they left. "See you at church."

"'Bye, Ed," Bradford answered. "S-s-s-see you, D-D-D-Dora," he yelled, shaking his rattles to annoy me.

By then we were too far away to hear Benjie's echo.

I wanted to shout, "Good riddance to bad rubbish!" to both of them, but I only muttered it to myself. I'm glad I didn't yell, because I stuttered on both "r"s.

The Lenstroms were the only family still with us when we passed through Clovis late that day. The town was nothing like Santa Fe. Both the people and the buildings looked more like the ones I was used to in Utah. As we rode past, I could hear English being spoken.

"Looks like the Lenstroms' homestead will be closer to ours than any of the others," Mama said.

"Looks like it," Papa replied.

"That's something to be thankful for," Mama said.

"Yup," Papa agreed. "We can give each other a hand now and then."

"And go for a v-visit," I added, "to play with J-Jenny and Sarah."

"How about camping at their place tonight?" Papa asked.

"Yes, yes!" Caroline said encouragingly. So we did.

It was nearly dark by the time the Lenstroms had located their homestead. Papa parked our wagon and we all jumped down to take a look at the house. I couldn't see much in the dim light, but I could tell there were two rooms. An old stove hunched in one corner.

Early the next day, we inspected the Lenstroms' farm. A dirt road ran around the edge of the property. Most of the land was knee-high in weeds. A well stood not far from the house, and a patch of dying vegetable plants showed where the garden had been.

"Looks like they had a crop," Papa said, kicking at some corn stubble.

"A small one," Brother Lenstrom agreed. "But there's plenty of room for a big one. Lots of other improvements to make, too.

But that's what we expected."

It wasn't what I expected. I was sure our place would be better.

"We need to be on our way," Papa said after we returned to the house. "The Williamsons will wonder where we are."

As Brother Talbot had predicted, the first person we asked knew where the Williamsons lived.

"Just four more miles along the road to Texico," he told us. "A white house with a red brick chimney on the left-hand side."

The minute Sister Williamson opened the door, I could smell the sage in the turkey dressing. Other delicious aromas came from the kitchen.

"My, my." Sister Williamson greeted us. "What a nice lot of helpers."

She asked us our names and ages, and when she got to me I said, "Dora, nine."

"How lucky for Lucy!" Sister Williamson said, "She just turned nine, too, and needs a friend her own age. Lucy," she called, "come meet Dora."

Lucy was lots taller than I was. She had long, brown braids and wore glasses. We looked at each other.

Finally she said, "Wanna sit by me on the piano bench?"

I nodded.

Evidently the Williamsons only had one child. The table was set for eleven, and there were eight of us Cooksons.

"I hoped you'd get here in time for dinner," Sister Williamson said. "As soon as I mash the potatoes and whip the cream, we'll be ready to eat. You can wash up on the back porch if you'd like."

When we were seated at the table, Brother Williamson called on Papa to say the blessing on the food. In honor of the occasion, he thanked God for every little thing he could think of. I thought he'd never quit praying. When he finally did, I was thankful for that.

We all ate as if we'd been saving our appetites for a month. It had been longer than that since we'd last eaten in a house. Our trip had taken fifty-three days.

After the meal was over and we'd cleaned up the kitchen, Papa asked Brother Williamson if he'd show us to our new home.

"You bet," he replied. "I'll saddle the horse and ride over with you. You might want to fill your water barrels first." He pointed to a well with a bucket.

When we climbed into our wagon, Papa was smiling. "We're almost there," he said, "to the place of our dreams."

CHAPTER THIRTEEN

DREAM OR NIGHTMARE?

Papa invited me to ride up front with him and Mama.

"You two were the first to hear about the homestead," he said. "It's only fair that you should be the first to see it."

We passed a few farms where cultivated land had been harvested and only stubble remained. Some fields had been plowed. Most of the land was still wild, covered with scrawny brush and the round clumps of spiky cacti that Brother Williamson called bear grass.

The route changed direction several times, and it was clear

that without help we would have had difficulty finding the homestead.

"There's the closest store," Brother Williamson said, pointing to a two-story building. "And that's the school across the street."

The school? I jerked my head around in a hurry to see a small wooden building that looked nearly new. It hadn't even been painted yet. It couldn't be more than one large room, I decided. I wondered how a whole school could fit into such a small place.

The sun hung low in the west when we first saw our homestead. It certainly didn't look like the lush, green, covered-with-watermelon Garden of Eden I was expecting. I don't know what made me think our place was going to be better than all the other farms around, but somehow I did. Instead, it was worse. It was nothing but a patch of weeds and bear grass.

Brother Williamson slowed his horse and pointed to a stick with red rag tied to it. "Your property begins at that stake," he told Papa. "It extends half a mile east, south, west, then north to make a square."

Papa looked over the parcel of land.

"Sure is level," he said. "No trees to clear off."

"It's a good piece," Brother Williamson said. "Needs a little work, is all."

Papa pulled on the reins to stop the horses and jumped down from the wagon. He kicked the cinnamon-colored soil with his boot, then picked up a handful and let it trickle through his fingers.

"Good sandy loam," he said. "Nothing better for growing crops." He looked toward some low hills in the distance.

"Don't see any mountains," he said. "Where does the water come from? I'm used to having streams pouring out of every canyon."

Brother Williamson laughed. "No canyons here," he said. "Or streams, either. You have to depend on the rain. But don't worry, there's usually enough for good crops."

"What about drinking water?"

"Most people have wells," Brother Williamson said.

"What happens if there's a drought?"

"Dries up," Brother Williamson said. "Same as any place."

"What do people grow around here?"

"Corn mostly. Milo, maize, kafir, and broom. You can sell all the broom corn you can grow to the factory over in Texico."

Papa walked along slowly, leading the horses and sizing up the property.

"Where's the house?" he asked.

"Around the bend in the road," Brother Williamson said, pointing ahead. "It's not very big. You'll have to add on. The Hoyts should be back from Texas in a week or so to pick up their things. Until then, you can start on the barn. There's a pile of lumber behind the house."

"There's no hurry for a barn in this warm country, is there?" Papa asked.

Brother Williamson laughed so hard he almost fell off his horse. "Where do you think you are?" he asked. "In Florida? Any day now we'll get a cold wind from the north, and you'll think you've moved to Alaska. The barn better be strong, or it will go down in the wind, and it better be tight or sand will blow through the cracks. Quick as a wink, the wind can change from north to south, warm everything up and melt the snow."

"Snow?" Papa, Mama, and I all asked at once.

"Oh, not much," Brother Williamson said, "but some every year. The altitude here is over four thousand feet, not much different from Salt Lake Valley. We have a long, hot growing season, but the winters are frosty."

"Let's see the house," Papa said and climbed back in the wagon. He *clucked* to the horses and they started up.

Soon after we turned the corner, we came to two tall, upright posts set far enough apart for a gate. The only sign of a fence was a roll of rusted barbed wire leaning against one of the posts.

"There it is," Brother Williamson said.

Mama gasped.

An unpainted shack was almost hidden in a tangle of weeds. Papa stopped the horses, and everyone climbed down from the wagon to take a closer look.

I couldn't believe it. A dirty-looking wreck of a house in the middle of a weed patch in another cold climate. Was this the answer to Mama and Papa's prayers? Their dream had turned into a nightmare.

I looked at Mama. Her mouth was set in a thin, hard line, and tears ran silently down her cheeks. Papa put an arm tenderly around Mama's shoulders and gave her a gentle squeeze. An empty, frightened feeling settled in the pit of my stomach.

Caroline could tell how awful I felt. "Don't worry, Dora," she whispered. "Papa will build us a new house and let us have that one to play in."

"I hope we c-can c-c-clean it up," I choked.

"Where are our temporary living quarters?" Papa asked Brother Williamson.

"It's only a dugout," he apologized, "but it's not too far away, and it's cozy."

He led us farther down the road toward some low, sandy hills. We came to another shabby shanty that looked even worse than the house. It wasn't much bigger than the wagon, in fact. A low roof sloped down to the ground on two sides. At one end were dirt steps that led to a sunken room that had been dug out of the ground. A small window in the opposite end gave the only light.

Brother Williamson offered to help Papa and Ed move our things in before he went back home, but Mama shook her head.

"Good night, then," he said, and rode off.

"I don't want anything in that dingy cave until I've cleaned out every corner," Mama insisted after he left.

"But not tonight," Papa said. "It's been a long enough day already."

"Yes," Mama agreed with a tired sigh, "at the end of a long, long journey."

"But it's still Thanksgiving," Papa reminded us. "We should remember to be thankful."

Even while Papa said the words, I wondered what there was to be thankful for in this dreary wilderness of weeds and cacti.

There was bread and warm milk from the cow for anyone who wasn't still full of turkey dinner, but my appetite was gone. We prepared to sleep out under the stars again.

The next morning Papa was singing when I woke up. I saw the look of trust that Mama gave him, and I knew everything was going to be all right after all. No matter how much work it took, we were going to have a place of our own.

Papa took Ed and me with him to look over our land and left Caroline and Frank to help Mama clean the dugout.

We walked around and across our quarter section. One spot wasn't much different from another. It was all flat, sandy and tree-less. In his mind Papa had already laid out the farm into orchard, pasture, cropland, vegetable garden, and corral. He showed Ed and me where each was to be.

"The house isn't as bad as it looks," he said, tramping around it through the weeds. "It's small and needs a coat of paint, but it's sturdy." He looked briefly in each direction. "New Mexico sure is different from Utah," Papa continued. "No rocks, no mountains, no trees, and no irrigation ditches. Not even any creeks with water. A bad drought could wipe out a crop."

My stomach felt hollow again.

Behind the house, almost buried by bear grass, we found a pile of lumber that had been there a long time.

"For the barn, I guess," Papa said.

Every once in a while, we came upon a deep hole in the sandy soil. Finally Ed asked what they were for.

"I've been trying to figure that out," Papa said, "and I've about decided they're probably places where the Hoyts tried to dig wells."

"Why so m-many?" I asked.

"Couldn't quit till they found water," Papa explained.

"Did they ever find it?" Ed asked.

"No," Papa said in a strange tone. "I don't believe they did. It seems to me that Brother Talbot said they got tired of hauling water to drink. I thought they were just too lazy to dig a well but it looks like . . ." Papa got a funny expression on his face and didn't finish the sentence for a long time.

Finally he said, "They probably didn't dig deep enough."

"P-pretty deep," I said, peering down one of the holes.

"But not deep enough," Papa repeated.

"What if *we* can't find water?" Ed asked.

"We'll find it," Papa promised us. I could tell he wasn't as confident as he tried to sound. "It *has* to be here," he insisted fiercely.

The scared, empty feeling in my stomach spread until it pushed my heart into a lump in my throat. Papa's bubbly excitement had gone flat, like bread dough falling after it has risen too high.

We headed slowly and silently back toward the dugout. Shortly before we got there, Papa stopped.

"I don't want your mama worrying about water," he said. "Do you understand?"

"Yeah," Ed replied. "I won't say anything."

"Dora?"

I nodded. I could feel my eyes get wet and my chin start to shake.

Papa grabbed me in a hug. "I don't want you worrying about it, either," he said.

"Maybe the Indian's stick can find it," Ed suggested.

"I'm counting on that," Papa said.

We arrived at the dugout just in time for the noon meal. It seemed like a different place from the one we'd left four hours before. Already, Mama, Caroline, and Frank had it looking and smelling like home. They'd cleaned up, found places for everything, and figured out where we all would sleep.

"You're a wonder, hon," Papa told Mama and gave her a kiss. "I'll build us a table and chairs first chance I get."

"No place to put them till we get into the house," Mama told him as she passed the sandwiches around. "We'll have to camp out for a while."

We ate outside in the sunshine, sitting on the sturdy quilt Mama had stitched together from pieces of overall material.

After dinner, we helped Papa get the stove off the wagon and into the dugout. He put the stovepipe through a hole in the roof and hooked it up where it belonged.

"All ready to use," he told Mama.

"Except for some fuel," she said. "There's no wood around here to burn—except packing boxes and barrels, and they won't be empty until we move into the house."

"I'll bring you some coal," Papa said. "There's part of a pile on our lot."

He picked up the shovel and a bucket for the coal.

"We found a few holes I need to fill before George and Howie fall in," he told Mama.

"Come on, Ed and Dora." He nodded at the witching wand the Indian had given him, and I knew that he meant for me to bring it.

When we walked onto our piece of land, Papa handed the shovel to Ed and reached for the stick. "Let's see that divining rod," he said to me with a wink. "It should be thirsty enough by now to find water. There's no time like the present to solve a problem."

"The convenient place for a well is behind the house," he said as we walked past. "We'll look there first."

"No holes here," Ed observed. "I wonder why."

"Probably filled them up," Papa said, "this close to the house."

Holding the branch horizontal to the earth with one prong in each hand and the other pointing straight ahead, Papa walked slowly around the area where he hoped to have a well.

Nothing happened. He tried again, shaking his head.

He moved gradually outward in a bigger and bigger circle, giving special attention to the places where digging had already been started. After he gave up on an empty hole, Ed and I took turns filling it with the light sandy soil.

When dusk came, Papa poked the stick into the ground to mark the place where he'd begin looking for water the next day. His shoulders sagged more than usual as we started back. I put a pretend smile on my face so Mama wouldn't figure out that maybe our Garden of Eden was really a waterless wilderness.

CHAPTER FOURTEEN

WHERE IS THAT WATER?

The next day Papa tried the water stick again, but it didn't work any better than the day before. We filled some more of the deep, dry wells. Ed and I pulled the weeds away from the woodpile while Papa marked the edges of the barn to begin building. Then Ed and I held the boards while he nailed them together. We saved the scraps to burn in the stove.

I knew that the barn was Papa's excuse for not digging the well first. As long as we were in the dugout, we had to haul water from the Williamson's, anyway.

Mama had noticed that Papa wasn't his usual happy self.

"You look peaked," she said. "You're working too hard."

"Well, tomorrow's a day of rest," he told her. "We'll go to Clovis to church. It's more than a ten-mile ride, though, so we need to start early."

While I unpacked my white Bible to take with me, I remembered how close the church was in Utah.

The meeting place was really a big house with enough rooms for classes of all ages. It was good to be in Sunday School again and to see most of the people we'd traveled with. We were welcomed warmly by the local Saints. They were delighted to have so many new people in the congregation. The Brownleys didn't come, and I was glad.

On the way home, we stopped at the Lenstroms' for dinner.

"I'm going to have this place fixed up in no time," Brother Lenstrom said. He showed Papa what he'd done already and told him what he planned to do next. I couldn't help being envious about how much nicer their place was than ours. I noticed the thirsty look in Papa's eyes when he inspected the well.

"Mind if I fill our barrels?" he asked Brother Lenstrom.

"Of course not," Brother Lenstrom replied. "Go right ahead."

"Our place doesn't have a well yet," Papa said. He didn't explain why.

Every day, no matter what else he did, Papa went out with the divining rod to try to locate water. He didn't say anything about it, but I could tell that he was becoming more and more frustrated.

"This is getting to be a nuisance," Mama complained every time the water barrel was empty. "When are you going to dig a well?"

"Pretty soon," Papa promised, warning me with a look.

After a week of useless off-and-on searching, Ed and Papa and I spent an entire afternoon walking around the property trying to find water. No matter who held the stick, it continued to point straight ahead without the slightest dip toward the ground.

"Where *is* that water?" Ed cried out.

"Only God knows," Papa said with a weary sigh.

"Wh-why not ask Him?" I said softly.

"What did you say?"

"Pray," I suggested.

"Of course!" Papa agreed. "That's the problem. I've depended so much on that Indian stick that I forgot all about asking God. I purposely didn't mention it in my prayers at home for fear I'd worry Mama."

We knelt down right where we were, and Papa poured out his heart to God as if he were talking to a friend.

When he stood up again, Papa was like a different man. He held the stick like it was a magic wand and started off as if he knew exactly where to go. Nothing had happened by suppertime, though.

"Maybe God's not going to answer your prayer," Ed said, worried.

"Oh, yes He is!" Papa insisted. "I could feel the way the stick pulled down while I was praying."

"Could you tell where?" Ed asked.

"Nope," Papa said, "I couldn't. We'll have to keep looking." He poked the rod in the ground at the edge of the lane near the house, and we started back to the dugout.

In the morning, Papa could tell the Hoyts were back when he spotted smoke coming out of their chimney. He and I hurried over to find out when they were moving. On the way, Papa picked up the witching wand.

Suddenly he stopped, took the stick in both hands and held it out in front of him. It trembled as if it were alive and tipped down toward the ground.

"Look at that, Dora," he said. "I think we've found water."

"Are you f-fooling me?" I asked.

"Not at all," Papa insisted. "All of a sudden I had this feeling that I was supposed to pay attention. Then something pulled the stick down. I didn't even have it pointed."

"Let me try."

I stood in exactly the same spot, and Papa placed two ends of the Y-shaped stick in my hands. The free end pulled toward the ground as if it had a rock tied to it.

"It works!"

"Yup," Papa agreed, taking the stick and trying it again. "It didn't ever do that before, but it sure does now."

"That's the m-middle of the lane," I said.

"Yup."

"You can't dig there."

"Oh, can't I?" Papa exclaimed gleefully. "I can jolly well dig anywhere there's water. We can move the lane. We may even have to move the house." Papa sounded as if he felt strong enough to do it with his bare hands.

"I never would have thought to try here," he said. "It seems like such a funny place to put up a water tank."

"Water tank?"

"Yes, to store the water."

Papa said "water" like he was mentioning gold. He was so happy he danced up to the Hoyt's door and knocked on it with a lively rat-a-tat-tat. He found out they would be gone the next day.

"We'll finish the barn today," Papa said, "so I can start digging the well as soon as they leave."

By evening, the animals were cozy inside the stable, and there was a pile of soft hay in the loft above. Ed and I begged to sleep there.

"Not until we move into the house," Papa said. "The barn's too far away from the rest of the family now."

The next day, Ed, Caroline, Frank, and I sat in the second-floor doorway of the barn loft watching the Hoyts pack up their wagon.

"I wish they'd hurry and go, so we can move in," Ed said.

"I wonder if they'll leave anything," Caroline said.

"P-p-prob'ly not," I predicted.

"The Lenstroms found all sorts of good things someone left in their house," Caroline reminded us.

"Like what?" I asked.

"A table and some fruit jars."

"And a pretty good harness," Frank put in.

"Don't forget the stove," Ed added. "They found a good stove."

"The oven has to be propped shut with a stick of wood," Caroline said, "or it falls down."

"It's still good," Ed insisted.

Finally, the Hoyts finished putting all their things into the wagon and started out the gate on their way back to Texas. It didn't seem possible that anything could be left in the house. We scrambled down the loft ladder and ran to look inside, anyway. There was just a single room and it was completely empty, except for one very important thing.

"A high chair!" Caroline exclaimed. "Look at that. Howie can have a high chair."

"That should keep him out of mischief at mealtime," Ed said.

"And while Mama cooks," Frank added.

"I wish they'd left a table," Caroline said. "That's what we really need. And some more chairs."

"Papa'll m-make some," I reminded her.

Mama was already coming through the door with her mop bucket full of sudsy water. Caroline parked Howie in the high chair to watch while she helped scrub down the walls. The rest of us went back to the dugout with Papa to move our things.

While Mama decided where everything went, Ed said, "I get to sleep in the barn."

"Me, too," I insisted.

"Nothing doing," Mama said. "The barn's for animals, not children."

"Papa promised," Ed told her.

"It's all right, hon," Papa told Mama. "The loft's clean and warm and close enough that we could hear them call if they needed us."

"You have a point," Mama agreed. "I guess it won't hurt to try it. We'll be stacked up like cordwood if all eight of us have to sleep in this one room."

Ed and I started out the door with a load of bedding. George grabbed onto my legs and shouted, "I wanna sleep with Dora! I wanna sleep with Dora."

"I don't think so," Mama said.

"I'll t-take c-care of him," I promised. "Let him come."

"Watch him, then, so he doesn't fall down the ladder," Mama cautioned.

"I don't fall down ladders," George said in a huff. "I climb down."

"That's good," Mama told him. "Then you won't get hurt."

After our beds were made, I carried my small wooden chest up to the loft.

Papa couldn't wait to start digging the well. He checked the location one more time with the witching wand and began shoveling dirt like he was expecting to find treasure. He was just getting a good start when Mama walked down from the house. "You're not putting the well there, are you?" she said.

"Yup," Papa said, "right here."

"In the middle of the lane?" Mama couldn't believe it. "In the front yard?"

"Yup."

"Why? It doesn't make any sense."

"It does if you've been through what I've been through to find water." Then he told her.

"I hope you've found it now," Mama said. She still didn't believe a witching wand could show Papa where the water was.

"Me, too," Papa agreed, and kept on digging.

CHAPTER FIFTEEN

CHRISTMAS IN NEW MEXICO

Papa hadn't been digging long when he sent Ed and me to get some boards to support the sides of the well so they wouldn't cave in. He stood the wooden slabs upright around the edge of the hole. We tapped them into the ground as the well got deeper and added new ones as they were needed. When Papa was too far down to toss the dirt out, he rigged up a bucket on a pulley. We wound it up, emptied the soil, and sent the empty bucket back for Papa to fill again.

Day after day, for nearly a week, he dug deeper and deeper

until the hole was three times as tall as he was, and still there was no water. His shoulders began to sag again, but he kept on digging.

One day Papa called up to me, "The ground's too hard for the shovel; send the pickax down in the bucket."

Slowly he chipped through a layer of shaley rock, and underneath the ground was sandy and moist.

"Hadn't better dig any deeper," he said when he climbed up out of the hole. "Water might come in fast enough to drown me before I can get out. I've heard some mighty scary stories about that. We'll just wait a while and see what happens."

He picked up the saw and said, "Who wants to go look for a Christmas tree?"

"I do!" Ed shouted.

"M-me, too," I said.

"I want to go," Frank insisted.

"Where can you find a Christmas tree?" Mama asked. "I haven't seen any pine trees growing around here. Or any trees, for that matter."

"Don't know," Papa said. "Maybe we'll have to use a cactus."

"A cactus Christmas tree?" Frank sounded disappointed.

"Why not?" Papa asked. "Think how pretty it would be with paper chains and popcorn strings hanging from the prickles."

"I guess so," Frank conceded.

"I'll pop some corn while you're gone," Mama said. "We'll string it when you get back."

We tramped around in the warm sunshine, trying to imagine it was winter. It seemed more like April than December.

"As soon as you see a good Christmas tree," Papa instructed us, "point it out and I'll cut it down."

We walked along the road in the direction of the sand hills. No trees grew anywhere.

"Can't you see any yet?" Papa asked.

"Ain't no trees here," Ed said.

"Aren't any," I corrected him.

"How about a tumbleweed?" Papa suggested and pulled a spiky round bush from next to the fence where the wind had tumbled it.

"Looks more like a snowball than a Christmas tree," Ed said.

"What's wrong with that?" Papa asked him.

"It's not tall enough," Frank complained. "It won't touch the ceiling."

"Look!" I exclaimed, pointing to a tall prickly green plant growing among the tumbleweeds.

Papa laughed. "I wondered when you'd notice," he said. "Those kosher weeds look just like junipers—perfect for Christmas trees."

"Not bad," Ed conceded.

"We can put it in a bucket of water," Papa said, "to keep it fresh."

"Let's find the biggest one," Ed said.

We finally agreed on a "tree" that was tall and full and almost perfectly cone-shaped. Papa cut it and put it across his shoulder to carry home.

"Now, let's get into the spirit of the season," he said encouragingly.

"How?" Ed wanted to know. "There's no snow."

"Let's see if we can think of enough different Christmas carols to last all the way home," Papa challenged.

"Silent Night," I suggested.

"Oh, Little Town of Bethlehem," Ed offered.

"The one about the wise men following yonder star," Frank said.

"That's a good one to begin with," Papa agreed. "We'll pretend we're the three kings traveling afar."

"And one queen," I insisted.

"Yes." Papa laughed. "Three wise men and one wise lady."

We filled the air with music, as our hearts filled with joy. I was especially happy because all the time I was singing, I didn't stutter at all. We hiked homeward in the bright desert twilight, bearing a prickly weed to decorate as our Christmas tree.

We draped it with popcorn strings. Then we made chains from the bright Christmas paper Mr. Younger had used to wrap our purchases in at the store. Mama had brought the shiny silver star for the top all the way from Utah.

There weren't many new playthings our first Christmas in New Mexico. Papa carved a little rolling pin for me, a top for Ed and something else for each of the other children. Mama sewed some new nighties, pajamas, and doll dresses. Santa Claus left a peppermint stick, a handful of nuts, and a strange orange fruit I'd never seen before in each of the stockings.

The painful experience with my tongue made me hate peppermint forever, so I gave mine to Ed. But I fell in love with the orange—the color, the shape, and the smell to begin with. It glowed like a bright sun sinking over the horizon and was rounded just right to fit the curve between my hands. The fragrance was mostly sweet, but a little bit bitter. Mama showed me how to peel it and divide it into sections to eat one at a time.

Oh, what delicious, sweet, sour, juicy goodness! I wanted more and more and more, a whole orange tree all for myself. As I finished the final segment, I closed my eyes and imagined a tree covered with orange balls like Christmas ornaments. It floated just above me in the sky—near enough that I could reach up and pick one any time I wanted to.

As wonderful as the orange was, the most exciting thing about that Christmas was something else.

Several times a day Papa had dropped a bucket down the deep well, hoping to hear a splash. The best he could get was damp sand sticking to the bottom. It had happened so often that none of us paid attention any more when Papa tried the well for water. But that morning, we all heard him scream and came running.

"*Eureka!*" he shouted. "I have found it! Eureka! Hallelujah! Hosanna and Hooray!"

He pulled the bucket out brimming over with water and set it down on the ground. Then he plunged both arms in and pulled them out to let the water run off.

"Water," he said quietly, as if the word were sacred. "Water."

I couldn't tell if he'd splashed his face or if it was tears that made it wet.

"That's the best Christmas present we could ever have," Mama said. She hugged Papa first and then all the rest of us. She picked up Howie last and whirled him around in a circle.

"We'll celebrate with pancakes for breakfast," she said.

"Hurry, then," Papa told her. "We have to get the pipe and sucker rods in."

"Come, Caroline," Mama said. "You can help me. Frank and George will set the table."

"What are sucker rods?" Ed asked, as soon as the others went inside.

"Those long wooden poles leaning against the barn," Papa told him. "They suck the water out of the ground."

"Where do you put them?" I wanted to know.

"First we put a big pipe down into the well," Papa explained. "Then we put the sucker rods, one at a time, inside that and push them down in the sand as far as they'll go."

"What if they aren't long enough?" Ed asked.

"We'll fasten another one onto the first," Papa said. "They're made so they can be screwed together."

"Then will the water come up?" Ed asked.

"Yes," Papa said, "and we'll need a windmill to pump it up into the storage tank."

"Why?" I asked.

"So we'll always have plenty of water," Papa said.

"Wh-where is the tank?" I asked.

"I ordered one from the Sears Roebuck catalog," Papa said. "It should be here in a week or two."

"Did you order a windmill, too?" Ed asked next.

"Nope," Papa said. "I'll have to build that."

By the time Papa had described the windmill, Mama was calling us for pancakes.

"With some of Grandma's good raspberry jam," she said.

"I didn't know we had any of that left," said Papa.

"I've been saving it for Christmas," Mama told him.

Papa had already hammered a table together and built benches so everyone could sit down to eat. Before long, our stomachs were as full of good food as our hearts were full of excitement.

As soon as the sucker rods were down in the well, Papa got busy building the windmill.

On New Year's Day, Mama reminded us that it was time for everyone to get back to school, now that Christmas vacation was over.

"You've missed too much already," she said.

Ed groaned, Caroline shrugged her shoulders, and I grinned from ear to ear. The very word *school* sent a prickle of pleasure up my spine. Now that I could speak, I planned to attend.

Late in the afternoon, I hummed happily as I polished my shoes on the back step. Mama came out and sat down beside me.

"We need to talk, Dora," she said.

"Okay," I agreed, noticing the cautious tone in her voice. "About what?"

"About school," she said.

"What about school?" I wondered. "It starts tomorrow."

"Yes," Mama said.

"And I c-c-can talk now, so I can go," I told her.

"Yes, you do very well," she agreed. "And yes, you *could* go, but . . ."

"But what?" I asked, not sure I wanted to hear her answer.

"You still stutter some," she said.

"N-not much," I insisted.

"You're right," she said. "Not much. But the problem with stuttering is that it gets worse and worse if people tease you about it. If you go to school . . . " She just shook her head like she knew what would happen there and grabbed me in a tight hug.

I tried to blink fast enough to keep the tears from spilling out.

"I know it breaks your heart not to go to school," she whispered in my ear. "But I keep thinking about cousin Mary. You wouldn't want to be like her, would you?"

I had forgotten all about cousin Mary, Ilene's older sister. She stuttered so much she never had a chance to finish a sentence because no one could stand to listen to her long enough. Someone else always completed her thoughts for her.

"No," I said quietly, "I d-don't want to be like that. But," I continued, my voice cracking with disappointment, "I w-want to go to school!"

"If you stay home a little longer, we can work hard on the stuttering," Mama persisted. "I'll borrow some books from the school and teach you to read so you won't be so far behind when you do start."

"I w-want to go now!" I told her.

"Very well," she agreed. "It might work out. If it doesn't, you can quit for a while."

"C-Cooksons aren't quitters," I said, quoting Papa.

"Not usually," she said, and returned to the subject of learning at home. "We could study every afternoon while the little boys take their naps. I saw a set of ABCs in Younger's window that would help you with writing and spelling."

"I am *going* to school tomorrow," I insisted stubbornly.

"It's up to you," she said. "In the meantime, think about what I've said."

It was getting dark, and Mama went back inside the house. But I couldn't. Not yet. Not feeling like a hollowed-out pumpkin shell with the lid jammed on tight to hold all the emptiness in. I needed to walk a while first.

I hated it when Mama told me to think about what she had said.

It always meant there was a wiser choice than the one I wanted to make. Well, this time I *wouldn't* think about it. My mind was made up. I intended to go to school.

I walked for a long time, trying not to think about Mama's suggestion—trying not to think about anything. The moon followed me, watching like a lopsided eye as I circled the homestead. Twice.

By then, I figured everyone would be asleep, but the lamp in the kitchen still flickered. I knew Mama was waiting up to tell me good night. I wasn't ready to talk to her yet, though, so I went to bed in the barn loft without going into the house.

I was still awake when I heard a quiet shuffling below me. The strong scent of homemade soap told me it was Mama, coming up to check on me.

I turned my back and pretended to be asleep, but I felt a warm tear touch my bare shoulder before she gently covered it with the quilt.

She left as quietly as she came.

It was the first time Mama had ever climbed the ladder to the loft.

CHAPTER SIXTEEN

ANOTHER SECRET

It wasn't Mama's tender concern that caused me to change my mind, but a nightmare.

I finally fell into a fitful sleep, tossing and turning throughout the night. I dreamed about how much I wanted to go to school. I saw myself walking through the open door, beaming with pride. Once I was inside, I tried to talk. The words came out in a tangled-up jumble, just as if cousin Mary were trying to say something. Then the taunting began. Jeering came from every corner of the classroom.

I woke with a start, glad I'd been dreaming. I knew I didn't want to start school like that. Mary never did learn to quit stuttering. Could I?

By morning I'd decided that any girl who'd taught herself to talk ought to be able to stop a stutter. I made up my mind to try out Mama's plan for a while and see how quickly I could do it.

When I came down from the loft wearing my old clothes, Mama could tell I'd changed my mind about going to school. She nodded briefly to indicate her approval.

I didn't feel like eating any breakfast, though, and the hollow place inside me grew bigger and bigger when Mama left with Caroline, Ed, and Frank to enroll them in school. I stayed sitting at the table with Papa, George, and Howie, staring straight ahead, not wanting to do anything.

Papa started right in to cheer me up with some silly nonsense.

"She sells seashells by the seashore," he said.

"So?" I asked in a lukewarm voice.

"So," he said, "'She sells seashells by the seashore' is a stutter stopper. If you learn to say it faster and faster, it will help get rid of all the extra letters that trip up your tongue."

We practiced saying the sentence together. George and Howie joined in. Before long, they were laughing.

Pretty soon Papa was saying some different words. "Skipping school, stopping stutters, she senses secrets sooner than her sis."

I started to repeat his new tongue twister before I recognized it as a message.

"What secrets?" I wanted to know.

"Can't tell secrets," Papa said mysteriously.

"P-p-please, Papa," I coaxed. He shook his head.

"Because you're home, you'll probably find out sooner than anyone else. But it's not time yet."

I knew Papa was trying to get me busy thinking about something so I'd quit feeling sorry for myself. His plan worked. It kept my mind alert, watching and listening for any kind of clue.

Knowing there was a secret and not knowing what it was was even worse than knowing one and not being able to tell it.

True to her promise, Mama brought a beginning reader back from the school. She left the little boys with Papa and took me to Younger's for the ABCs.

When we got to the store, the letter cards were still on display. Mr. Younger pulled out a new box and told Mama the price.

"Oh, dear," she said, "I didn't think they'd be that much."

What if we didn't have enough money?

"I could let you have the ones in the window for less," Mr. Younger said. "Some are faded a little and the box is lost, but all the letters are there—both upper and lower case."

"That will be fine," Mama said.

"Are they for the little lady here?" the storekeeper asked. "I know just the thing to put them in so she won't lose any."

He climbed his tall ladder, got a flat box down from a high shelf, and brushed it across his pant leg to get rid of the dust. Then he slipped the cards inside and handed it to me. It was a beautiful box with a picture on the lid of an elegant lady in a wide-brimmed hat.

"You can make words till the cows come home," he told me.

That's exactly what I intended to do. I knew right where I was going to hide the box so no one would disturb it. Underneath the window ledge by my bed was a space between two boards just big enough to stand it on end. I'd put my pillow and a folded quilt in front so George wouldn't be tempted to get into it and lose some of the letter cards.

Every afternoon, Mama helped me learn to read some of the words in the school book. When she taught me how to sound them out, I found out right away how important Ed's help with the ABCs had been. After Mama and I had our lesson together, I went up to the barn loft and spelled out the words we'd been studying with my letter cards. By the next day, I knew them.

One day, George and Howie slept so late that Mama and I were still working when Frank came home from school.

"Hey," he said, "that's the same book I use at school."

"That's right," Mama agreed. "It's the first grade book. You and Dora can read it together."

I'd never thought about being in first grade before. It might not seem like much to most people. But it was an important beginning for me.

In the mornings, while Mama was busy in the house, I worked outside with Papa. He knew all sorts of tongue twisters, and we practiced them together.

Peter Piper picked a peck of prickly pickled peppers.

How much wood would a woodchuck chuck if a woodchuck could chuck wood?

The shortest one, *Bumpy rubber buggy bumpers,* was the hardest to say without getting mixed up. No wonder Papa's sentences were called tongue twisters. They tangled my tongue in knots. We recited them together while we worked—slowly at first, gradually increasing the speed. I found that when I said the words at the same time Papa did, it was easy not to stutter. When

I tried the sentences alone, it was hard.

Sometimes Papa made up new tongue twisters about what we were doing.

The day he put the finishing touches on the top of the windmill, he called down,

"Windmill, windwheel, waterwheel whirl,
Waterwheel, windwheel, windmill whir,
Whirl, whir, whirl, whir, whirl, whir, whirl."

We repeated the twister a couple of times, then he said, "Now go into the house and get your mama."

When we came out, Papa was hanging upside down from the highest cross piece. "Look, hon!" he shouted. "It's all finished."

Mama looked up and gasped.

"Albert B. Cookson, you come down here right this minute before *you're* finished. You'll have every last one of these youngsters thinking they can do crazy antics like that up there. Before you know it, someone will fall and break his neck."

Papa flipped easily to his feet, climbed down, and ran over to silence her with a kiss.

"You worry too much," he said.

"No wonder, with such a loony husband," she scolded, trying not to smile. "You scared me half to death."

After Mama went back into the house, I started to climb the windmill to try Papa's trick.

"No, you don't!" he cried, and grabbed me from below. "Mama's right about the danger. What you children need is an acting pole."

"What's that?" I asked.

"It's a horizontal bar to climb on, to swing from, to hang by your knees, or to do any other fancy tricks you can think of," Papa explained. "Some people call it a 'tricky bar.' I'll build you one right now with some of the lumber and pipe left over from the windmill."

"How?" I asked.

"Simple," he said. "Two posts in the ground with a pipe between."

"Is that the secret?" I asked.

"Nope," he said, "but it's an advantage of staying home. You'll have the first chance to try it out."

Papa sawed two square posts taller than he was. Then he measured and marked three places about a foot apart toward one end of each.

"What for?" I asked.

"To drill holes to slide the pipe through," he explained.

"Why in three places?" I asked.

"To make it adjustable," he said, "so it fits any size child from *C* to *H*."

I knew he meant from Caroline to Howie.

He dug two deep holes, set the posts, tamped the dirt tightly around them, and slipped the pipe into place. Soon I was copying Papa's trick at a safe distance from the ground.

The picture I drew for my sampler, though, showed Papa hanging by his knees from the top of the windmill.

His next project was to build a platform to hold the water tank he'd ordered.

When Papa got the notice it had arrived in Texico, I went with him to pick up the boxes that held the pieces we needed to assemble.

We unpacked all the parts and spread them out on the ground near the platform.

"I'm glad an instruction book was included," Papa said. "That's a lot of pieces."

We sorted them into groups.

"Papa picked a polished part and placed it in a pile of pegs," he sang.

"How about, Peter piper picked a piece and put it in a perfect place?" I asked.

We continued thinking of *P* words until we'd finished our project.

It took the help of all the family, as well as the Lenstroms and Williamsons, to assemble the tank and put it in place on top of the platform. They pressed and poked and plugged and pounded before it was perfected.

"Why does it have to be so high?" Ed asked, as the men struggled to lift it.

"So the water can run downhill," Papa explained.

Before long everything was connected. The pump, run by the windmill, sucked the water out of the well and poured it into the tank. A pipe that ran down from the tank had a handy spigot to turn the water on and off when we needed it. Papa's grin was as wide as a watermelon wedge.

"A farmer always feels better with a water supply," he said. "Now we can get the orchard planted. I saw bare-root fruit trees for sale at the farm supply store."

I helped him choose which kinds to buy. He decided to get one for each of us children.

"You'll have your own tree to take care of," he told me, "and when the fruit is ripe, you can share it with everyone else."

"I want an orange tree," I said.

The clerk shook his head. "Oranges don't grow here," he said. "It's too cold. You need to live in Florida or California to have oranges."

I settled for an Early Harvest apple tree.

"Are the fruit trees the secret?" I asked Papa.

"Nope," he said.

"What then?"

"Can't tell yet," he said.

The orchard was no sooner planted than a frigid north wind blew down from Alaska.

"Will the new trees freeze?" I asked Papa.

"No," he assured me. "They need to have cold feet in the winter or they won't bear fruit in the fall. But our fingers will freeze if we work outside. Why don't we stay in the barn and make some more furniture?"

"Good idea," I replied.

"I think I'll build a sofa," he said, "so we'll have a place to sit when company comes. Mama will fix some cushions to make it soft and Caroline can use it to sleep on at night."

"Is that the secret?"

"Nope. After that, I'll make a trundle bed for Frank and Howie. It will slide under the big bed to keep it out of the way during the day."

"Is that it?"

"Nope."

Papa could keep a secret better than anyone I ever knew.

CHAPTER SEVENTEEN

THE SINGING SPRING

One afternoon Mama didn't feel very well, so I studied by myself in the barn loft. I heard the door below open and close quietly. A soft rustle came from Papa's workroom. Whatever he was doing in there, he wasn't making much noise. Maybe it had something to do with the secret. I went down to find out.

Papa was weaving a big oval basket. The sides sloped out a little, and the top was nearly finished. The braided edge turned into a small handle on each side. It looked pretty fancy for a wash basket.

"Whatcha making?" I asked.

"Basket," he said.

"What for?" I wanted to know.

"Mama," he answered.

"She know about it?" I asked.

Papa shook his head. "Surprise," he whispered.

So that was the secret. Another basket for Mama. What was exciting about that? Disappointment dragged down on my shoulders and made them sag.

"What for?" I asked, not really caring.

Papa smiled and, calm as anything, said, "The new baby."

"*The new baby?*" I squealed. "Really? Truly?"

"Really, truly," he said. "But I wouldn't yell out a secret if I were you."

"How do you know?" I whispered.

"I just know," he whispered back.

"How?" I repeated.

"I just do," he said in his that's-something-too-special-to-talk-about voice.

I decided to try another question.

"When?" I asked.

"Pretty soon," he told me. "Isn't that exciting?"

"Oh, yes! Yes! Yes! Yes!" I hugged him so tight he pulled my arms away from his neck.

"You're choking me," he gasped, and I loosened my grip.

"Boy or girl?" I whispered in his ear.

"Don't know," he told me.

"I hope it's a sister," I said. I'd hoped for a sister ever since Elizabeth Ann Owens was born on the way to New Mexico.

"Well, don't hope it out loud," Papa warned me. "Remember, a secret is a secret."

"Does anyone else know?" I asked.

"Only Mama," he said.

"I won't tell," I promised. It was nice to know I *could* tell if I needed to.

I was afraid my face would give the secret away. Such happiness as I felt seemed impossible to hide. I imagined it shining from my skin like a warm glowing halo. Mama noticed the difference.

"That's pretty happy humming for a girl who's washing the dishes," she observed.

"Mm-hmm," I answered and kept on humming. I was planning my own surprise. I wanted to make something for the baby, something as soft and cozy and lovely as the secret I was carrying in my heart. Like the doll shawl I had given to Ilene.

After I finished the dishes, I went to see what leftover yarn I could find to crochet a coverlet. There wasn't enough to make anything. I did find some fresh flannel scraps in the rag bag, however. Mama must have been sewing new baby clothes while I was busy helping Papa.

I decided to cut out some squares and sew them together into a little quilt. I embroidered a yellow daisy in each of the blocks except the center one. In that one I put the initials *IC*.

Maybe the new baby could have the same name as my friend back in Utah—Ilene. Or Isabel. Or maybe Ina. I didn't want to think that maybe the baby might be an Ira or Isaac or Irving.

I made the back of the quilt from the calico scraps left over from my Sunday dress. The baby would like looking at the bright colors. I had to ask Mama for some cotton batting to put in the middle and she wanted to know what I was making.

"Something for a little doll," I told her.

I spread the flat sheet of cotton between the top and bottom of the quilt like a slice of ham in the middle of a sandwich. Then I tied yellow yarn bows through the corners of each block to keep the filling where it belonged. After I finished the edges of the quilt, I held it up to my cheek to try out the softness. It was perfect. I tucked it in the basket in the barn and waited for the baby to come. How soon was pretty soon? It had been a week since Papa told me what was going to happen.

Waiting for a secret to happen is even worse than all the knowing, not knowing, or not telling. The days seem to get longer and longer, like taffy stretched between the fingers.

I could tell that Mama was getting anxious, too. I still had all those questions I wanted to ask her about how babies got here from heaven, but I had promised Papa I wouldn't talk about the secret, so I saved them for later.

On Valentine's Day, I was helping George and Howie cut out red paper hearts when Mama said, "Sister Williamson has invited you and the boys over to make some cookies."

"Goody!" I said, jumping up from the table.

"If I let you go, can you watch George and Howard so they won't be any bother?"

All of a sudden, Howie had become Howard. Mama had been referring to him as "my little man" a lot lately and telling him how big he was growing. It seemed to me it should be clear to everyone that he wasn't going to be the baby of the family much longer. If anyone else had guessed the secret, they didn't let on.

I was eager for any break in the monotony of waiting and wondering when it would happen. A morning in the sweet-smelling Williamson kitchen was as tempting as a carrot to a pony.

"Will I be able to stay until Lucy gets home from school so we can play house?" I asked.

"Maybe," Mama told me. "Depends on when Papa can come to get you."

I took my doll, Henrietta, just in case. Lucy had all sorts of child-size furniture that her daddy had made. It was arranged like a playhouse in a corner of their kitchen.

Mama helped to settle the boys in the wagon and waved as we drove away. Papa was as jolly as a jaybird, singing and hurrying the horses along as if we were late for a picnic.

When we got to our friends' house, he jumped down from the wagon seat, lifted the boys out, said a few words to Sister Williamson, and was gone.

By the time Lucy got home from school, dozens of warm cookies were spread out on brown paper all ready to eat. I had set the small table for a play dinner and Sister Williamson poured milk into the toy cups. Before we even had a chance to take one bite, Papa drove up in front of the house and called to me. I went out to the wagon.

"I'm not ready to go home yet," I told him.

"Not even to see the Valentine surprise?" he asked.

"You mean the baby's here?"

"Yup," Papa told me, "about one o'clock."

I'd missed it again! Mama had arranged for us children to be gone when the new baby came. She'd done the same thing when George and Howie were born.

"Is it a . . . "

"Girl? Yes, a little angel with dimples and yellow hair, just like yours. We decided to name her Irene because that means *peace*. With such a big family, we need a peaceful baby."

Irene. Almost the same as *Ilene,* but not exactly. Irene. That was more beautiful than any of the names I'd thought of. Just imagine, a little girl who looked like me. It seemed too good to be true. What do you say when a secret turns out even better than you'd ever imagined? I couldn't think of a thing.

"Well, don't just stand there with your mouth open," Papa said. "Go tell everybody!"

So I did. I was so excited that I stuttered a lot, but I was able to make George, Howard, Lucy, and Sister Williamson understand that we had a new little 's-s-sister.'

The boys and I climbed quickly into the wagon to go see her. Sister Williamson handed us some cookies to eat on the way and Papa flipped the reins and clucked to the horses to hurry up.

It seemed like the ride home took lots longer than usual because I was so anxious to see the baby. Finally we got there, and I flew into the house to find Mama in bed, cuddling a soft little bundle wrapped in the quilt I'd made. Irene's tiny face peeked out as pretty and small as a baby doll's. Mama let me hold her and I touched her soft-as-silk hair to my cheek. At that instant, I was glad to be having school at home. Soon I'd be reading stories to Irene.

I still had the baby in my arms when Caroline, Ed, and Frank came in the door. The boys were both surprised and pleased about a little sister, but Caroline just said, "Well, finally," and reached to take her turn holding Irene. I wondered how long she had known the secret.

"Nice quilt," she said.

"Yes," Mama agreed, "it's beautiful. Dora made it."

Caroline looked at me as if to ask, "How did *you* know?" but kept the question to herself.

The new basket for the baby didn't fit anywhere. Sometimes it sat on the sofa, sometimes on the floor, and sometimes on the dinner table. All day long it was shifted from one place to the other to get it out of the way of what was going on.

One day when Papa was moving it again for the fourth or fifth time, he said, "This house isn't big enough. We're bursting at the seams. I'd better add on a room."

As usual, when he thought of a project, he was ready to get on with it. Before long, he had another room built next to the one the family lived in. He cut out the door between them and suddenly the house was twice as big. It seemed like a palace with a kitchen *and* a bedroom. Now the baby could sleep without being disturbed. Everyone enjoyed the extra room, but Ed, George, and I were still happy to have our beds in the barn loft.

Having a new baby didn't keep Mama from giving me lessons every afternoon. Now, she just nursed and rocked Irene while I read to both of them. Often, while the baby slept, I read the stories to George and Howard.

I was so happy to have a baby in the house that I sang all spring. I sang as I swished Irene's clothes clean in the sudsy water. I sang as I hung them out to dry. I sang soothing lullabies when I rocked her to sleep at bedtime and lively nursery rhymes while I tickled her toes and clapped her hands together.

When I sang, I didn't stutter. Something about the way the words fit into the tune didn't leave room for any extra sounds and, when there was no room, I didn't say them. I still stuttered some on words that weren't set to a melody, however. So Papa and I said the tongue twisters over and over.

I had a lot of helpers while I was getting ready to go to school. Mama taught me to read. Papa worked on my stutter. George, Howard, and baby Irene listened to the stories. Even Frank made my preparation easier. We took turns reading the first grade book to each other.

CHAPTER EIGHTEEN

NOT ENOUGH HOURS

While Mama and I were busy with school and the baby, Papa was hard at work clearing off the weeds and breaking the ground to plant a crop of broom corn. He plowed a place near the house for Mama to have a vegetable garden.

Papa watched the moon as well as the weather. He insisted that root crops should be planted in the "dark of the moon," and crops that matured above ground, when the moon was full.

"Why?" I asked.

"My dad taught me to," he said, as if that were reason enough.

"I don't know why exactly, but the right timing is supposed to make everything grow better."

I had no idea how much work a big garden would be when I helped Mama plant hers just before school was out. Back in Utah, we had a small family garden. Grandpa had one big enough to supply us with anything extra we needed. Now we were on our own.

Mama had every kind of vegetable seed she could beg, borrow, or buy. We planted row after row of beans, beets, peas, turnips, carrots, spinach, chard, squash, radishes, lettuce, tomatoes, potatoes, parsnips, cucumbers, and sweet corn. And a great big watermelon patch.

By the time school ended, the seeds were sprouting so fast we had to start on the weeding and thinning. That was only the beginning. For the rest of the summer, work on the homestead kept all of us busy all of the time.

The rain came at just the right times to keep the crops thriving. Papa's broom corn grew in straight green rows. We pulled out the weaker plants and stripped off the short suckers that shot up from the roots.

"They just use up energy that should go to the top," Papa explained.

The stalks were as high as my chin the day Papa pulled three white crayons from his pocket. He handed them to Ed, Caroline, and me.

"I want you to draw a line around the bottom of each of the cornstalks," he told us and showed us how.

"What for?" Caroline wanted to know. She hated to work outside and needed to be convinced her effort was necessary.

"To keep the ants from crawling up," Papa told her. "They won't cross that greasy line."

"Will ants hurt the corn?" I asked.

"No, but aphids will," Papa told us. "And where there are ants, there are aphids."

"Why?"

"The ants move them from place to place to be their cows."

"Cows?" Ed asked.

"Yup," Papa said, "the ants milk them."

"How?" Ed wanted to know.

"They stroke the aphids' backs and lick up the sweet fluid that comes out. One little aphid can't do much damage to a cornstalk, but they multiply so fast that before you turn around twice, the whole plant is covered. Before long, all its strength is sucked away."

"Do we have to do all of them?" Caroline asked with a groan.

"Every plant," Papa said. "If each of you does three rows a day, the job will soon be finished."

"Three rows!" Ed complained. "That's impossible."

"Okay, two then—to start with," Papa compromised. "Now, get to work."

I looked at the corn patch. All I could see was a solid green field. But I knew how long the rows stretched out. I had walked along dropping the seeds into the holes as Papa dug them. There were thousands of sturdy stalks to circle with crayons—maybe even millions.

"It will take forever," Caroline grumbled.

"Oh, no, not forever," Papa promised. "Only a week or two."

The first day seemed like forever. It was horrible. Our backs hurt long before we were done. The rows seemed to go on for miles. No one finished two. We were so tired at the end of the day we could hardly force ourselves to walk to the house. We fell into bed as soon as supper was over.

The next day was worse. When Ed tried to figure out where to start, he couldn't tell which plants had been done. The heat had melted the crayon marks and they were invisible.

"All that work and you can't even tell we did it," Ed grumbled.

"I hope Papa can," Caroline said.

"I hope the ants can," I added.

"We won't forget to mark where we stop today," Ed said.

Our backs never quit aching. The third day was worse than the first two. We all complained to Papa.

"It's a hard job, all right," he agreed, "but pretty soon your muscles will quit complaining. Before long they'll be so strong you won't even notice you're working."

"I doubt that," Ed grumbled.

"Me, too," Caroline agreed.

"Wait and see," Papa advised.

He was right, as usual. Just when I thought I couldn't live through another day of bending over and drawing around cornstalks, the pain began to ease. By the time the chore was finished, I had worked out a rhythm that made the job easy and efficient. Standing between two rows, with a crayon in each hand, I reached out in both directions to circle two stalks at once. Then I took a step backward to take care of the next pair.

I imagined my hands were dancing the same step over and over—a loop around the stem and a line to the next plant. A loop and a line, a loop and a line. I planned to embroider that double-track design on my sampler.

While I worked, I sang another tongue twister I'd made up so I could get rid of my stutter.

"Crayons circle cornstalks, crayons circle cornstalks." I repeated the refrain faster and faster as I speeded up my actions to keep up with the tempo. I soon got ahead of both Ed and Caroline. On the last day, I helped them finish their rows.

"Now," Papa said, "you need to do the sweet-corn patch." He had been careful to plant the two varieties of corn at some distance from each other. Brother Williamson had warned him that if they cross-pollinated, the table corn would be hard enough to break our teeth.

I watched the watermelon vines as more and more scalloped gray green leaves grew on each stem. Soon the plants sprawled in every direction, and small, yellow, star-shaped blossoms opened out. The flowers seemed all the same to me until Mama showed me that some of them were different from the others.

"This one," she said, choosing a bloom with a small green blob below it, "will turn into a melon after a bee brings it some golden grains of pollen."

"Where does the bee get it?" I asked.

"From the stamens of this other kind of flower," Mama explained, touching the center, where several yellow strands stood erect. When she lifted her finger, it had some of the powdery pollen on it.

"Just in case the bees haven't found the patch yet," Mama said, "you can get some early fruit if you transfer the pollen with your finger."

"You mean I can be the bee?" I asked.

"Exactly," Mama replied, touching the center of the fruit flower with her yellow fingertip.

Once the garden started to produce, there was no way to turn it off. Mama was determined not to waste a bit of it. What we couldn't eat, we put away for winter. We bottled, pickled, and dried vegetables until I didn't want to see the next day begin. No matter how long the sunny summer days stretched out, there were not enough hours to finish all the work.

When the neighbors told Papa they had extra fruit in their orchards, he sent us to pick it, and we bottled that, too. If anyone complained, Mama said, "You won't grumble next winter when you're enjoying the delicious flavor."

We all got busier and busier. Papa was so tired one Saturday night that he said he didn't even want to think about driving over to Clovis for church the next day.

"The horses need a day of rest as much as we do," he sighed. "We'll have Sunday School at home tomorrow."

I couldn't believe we'd miss going to church for any reason. Papa must have been really exhausted.

The next morning, Mama insisted that we dress in our Sunday best for our Bible study at home. We sang a hymn, Mama said a prayer, and Papa taught the lesson. I really missed going to Clovis, though, especially having Sunday dinner with the Lenstroms.

In the end, we stayed away from church for several weeks. By then, we'd quit dressing up. We even went barefoot, the same as every day.

Any time Papa could spare from working in the fields, he spent fixing up the house. First, he dug a big hole for a basement. In one part he built shelves so there would be a place to store the bottled fruit. In another corner he made a root cellar to keep carrots, potatoes, and parsnips after they were dug in the fall. He boarded off an area for a coal bin and fixed a window with a chute so he could fill it from the outside. Over the basement, he built a front room, where Caroline slept on the sofa, and a porch. Ed, George, and I still enjoyed sleeping in the hayloft. The house faced a different direction by then, so the water tank was at the side instead of in front.

One Saturday I went to Texico with Mama to buy some more fruit jars, and we met Sister Williamson and Lucy in front of the hardware store.

"Why, Betty Cookson," Lucy's mother said, "I haven't seen you in a month of Sundays. Hope no one's been sick so you couldn't come to church."

"No, we're fine," Mama assured her. "Albert's been working the horses pretty hard and he says they need a day of rest on Sunday even more than we do. When we get another team he'll trade off, and then we can drive into Clovis for church."

"Is that all? Why don't we just stop by and pick you up then?"

"Oh, no, that's too much trouble."

"No trouble at all. Our wagon's plenty big and you're right on the way. Besides, Lucy will be glad to have a friend to go to Sunday School with."

I really wanted to attend church again. As much as anything, I was anxious to get away from the never-ending summer work. Cucumbers grew on Sundays the same as any other day, and had to be picked. They'd be too big by Monday.

"Please, Mama," I coaxed.

"Maybe the girls could go," Mama said. "The boys don't have any shoes right now. Can't afford fruit trees *and* shoes. We needed to get the orchard in this year."

"That's right," Sister Williamson agreed. "First things first."

So that was the *real* reason we stayed home from church. The boys had outgrown their shoes. We must be getting short of money. No wonder we had to bottle all the food we could while it was growing in the garden.

"We'll stop by for Caroline and Dora then," Sister Williamson said. "About nine o'clock tomorrow morning."

"We'd be very grateful," Mama told her.

When I tried on my Sunday dress that night, it was too short.

"I need to add a piece on the bottom," Mama said. "You're growing as fast as the Christmas-tree kosher weeds along the fence rows."

I reminded Mama that I'd used the cloth that matched my dress for the back of Irene's quilt. Mama made a white ruffle of the only material she could find—a bleached flour sack.

Caroline's Sunday shoes pinched her toes, but she didn't tell Mama. She was as eager as I was to get dressed up and go somewhere.

We were ready and waiting long before the Williamsons drove into the yard to pick us up. I was so happy to be going to church that I hugged my Bible and hummed hymns all the way.

I saw the Brownley brothers as soon as I climbed down out of the wagon in Clovis.

"Well, well," Bradford said, "look what the cat dragged in."

"Yeah," Benjie agreed.

"So some of the Cooksons finally decided to come to church, did they?" Bradford continued.

"Finally," Benjie echoed.

"Where's Ed?" Bradford asked.

"Yeah, where's Ed?" Benjie repeated.

"Home," Caroline said.

"How come?" Bradford wanted to know.

"He's busy." Caroline wasn't about to say he didn't have any shoes.

"Workin' on Sunday?" Bradford asked.

"Breakin' the Sabbath?" Benjie said accusingly.

"No, not breaking the Sabbath," Caroline replied in an icy tone of voice that made Bradford decide to change the subject.

"Did Dumb Dora ever learn to talk without stuttering?" he asked Caroline as if I were not even there.

"Yeah, can she talk yet?"

I was so disgusted that I answered for myself. "Of c-c-c-course I c-c-c-can!"

I couldn't believe how the words came out. I thought I'd stopped stuttering completely. I was looking forward to starting school in September. Now I found out that the minute I got nervous the words trembled on my tongue like I was shivering with a chill. My face burned as hot as fire, and Bradford decided to fan the flame.

"Of c-c-c-course you c-c-c-can." He laughed.

Then Benjamin chimed in with his annoying echo. "Of c-c-c-course you c-c-c-can!"

What happened next surprised me even more than my stuttering had.

Caroline stepped forward and glared right in Bradford's face.

"YES, SHE CAN!" she yelled. "Dora can talk all she wants to without stuttering at all!"

Bradford backed away, shocked.

"And what's more," my sister continued, shaking her finger in front of Benjie's nose, "she doesn't need any bratty smart alecks talking about her like she's not even here. She *is* here. Now, leave her alone. DO YOU UNDERSTAND?"

Both boys ducked their heads and held their hands in front of their faces as if to say, "Please don't hit us, we surrender."

Caroline didn't need Ilene's quick fists. She did the job with her tongue. My sister had shown me how to handle bullies without fighting. I decided I needed to practice her method before school started. And I needed to do it without stuttering.

CHAPTER NINETEEN

THE OPEN DOOR

Finally, the watermelons were ripe. It was the best thing about the farm. I loved the crisp, cracking sound when the knife bit into the green shell and spread open the luscious fruit. Colored like a rosebud, it was speckled with flat, shiny, black seeds, just right for spitting target practice. My face was always sticky from being buried in a piece of watermelon.

Best of all, no one had to bottle, dry, pickle, or preserve melons. They were just for enjoying while they were fresh, juicy, and sweet. I'd heard of watermelon-rind preserves and was afraid

Mama might decide to make some. But she didn't.

"Summer'll be gone before we know it," Papa said one day in August. "I see they're cleaning up the school grounds and even painting the building. That new teacher must be a real go-getter."

"His name would choke a horse," Mama complained. "It's bad enough to keep Dora stuttering all day."

"What's his name?" I asked.

"McLaughlin," she said. "Mister McLaughlin."

She was right. It was hard to say. *M* was the easiest letter to stutter on, and saying the other part of the teacher's name was like stirring a mouthful of mashed potatoes with my tongue.

But having a problem is one thing, and doing something about it is another. It was time I got on with a solution. The first day we dried corn, I began to practice.

Except for watermelon, nothing is so deliciously sweet as corn on the cob fresh from the garden. The eight-row variety we grew had the kernels spaced just right to bite off easily—four sections with two rows in each.

I loved to walk down the whispering rows with Papa to pick enough for dinner while Mama got the pot of water boiling to cook it. If the ear felt full and hard with the silk frizzled brown on top, it was ready. Papa grabbed it firmly and cracked it off with a quick downward jerk.

Sometimes there was a little baby ear of corn growing right next to the big cob. The pink or green cornsilk looked like long hair, and tender husks were wrapped around the tiny body like a blanket. Once in a while, there were twin corn babies. I always saved these little dolls and made cradles for them to sleep in.

When the corn patch was at its peak of production, Ed and Papa carried bushel after bushel into the shade by the house so

Frank and I could husk it. Mama sliced off the kernels with a sharp knife and tossed the cobs to the chickens. They ran for the treat, flipped up their feather-duster behinds, and dropped their heads to peck up the corn worms and clean off the cobs.

Caroline put the prepared corn in shallow baking pans and heated it for a while in the oven. Then she spread the steaming kernels on flour-sack dish towels to dry in the sun. Flies swarmed around the fragrant sheets but couldn't get through the mosquito netting that was secured across the top to keep them out. After several hot days, with occasional stirring, the corn was hard and dry. We stored it for winter use in cloth bags hung from the rafters so mice couldn't get to them.

Nothing was wasted. The husks were dried to save for filling mattresses and quilts, the cobs stacked in a pile to use for fuel.

I could remove the husk from an ear of corn with two quick pulls, one with each hand. I decided to practice the schoolteacher's name to a tune while I did it.

"Mister," I sang, as I ripped half the husks away with my right hand. "McLaughlin," I crooned, zipping to the left.

"Mister"—*rip*—"McLaughlin"—*zip*. I repeated the name over and over as I stripped the cobs and tossed them into the dish pan for Mama. Only if I hesitated did a stutter sneak in.

The corn patch looked pretty bedraggled after we'd harvested most of the ears. The jaunty, brightly colored scarecrow that hung on a fence post to frighten the birds away had done a good job. Papa decided to save it for next year. He suspended it from a hook in the barn right next to the ladder to the loft. It grinned at me every time I went up or down. I decided to pretend it was the schoolteacher.

"Good morning, Mister McLaugh–lin," I sang as I passed it.

Or "Good afternoon, Mister McLaughlin," or "Good night, Mister McLaughlin."

I was determined to be in the classroom this year. I knew that if I stuttered, Mama would think I should stay home again.

I practiced my greeting over and over until I could say it without singing. On the other side of the ladder, I nailed a rusty pie plate with a painted frown and pretended it was Bradford Brownley. Remembering his teasing made me mad enough to tell him off, like Caroline had done. I found out that I didn't stutter at all when I was angry. I didn't need to worry that the Brownley boys would be in my class, because they lived too far away to go to the same school. But there was bound to be a bully in Mr. McLaughlin's room.

August moved right along toward my tenth birthday on the twenty-ninth. Soon school would be starting again. Could I convince Mama that I was ready to go?

I didn't expect the answer to my question to be wrapped up in a box and handed to me for a birthday present, but it was. Inside were a blue calico dress and a pair of new shoes. The only possible thing I could need them for was school.

I didn't know how to act when the dream of my life was about to come true. I always thought I would climb up on the windmill, wave my arms around with the blades and shout, "Hooray!"

I could picture my voice flying around in the whir and spinning off in a breeze. It would carry my excitement out into the air for all the world to hear.

"I'm going to school . . . Going to school . . . to school . . . school . . ."

Instead it seemed that my voice was closed off by a hard lump that felt like my heart had jumped up in my throat. A silly tear trickled down my cheek, and my chin trembled.

"Hey," Papa said, "it's nothing to cry about. I thought you wanted to go to school."

"I do," I whispered. "Oh, I do."

"Then smile about it," Mama suggested, and I lifted the corners of my quivering lips.

Later in the day I walked by myself over to the schoolhouse and looked at the newly painted door that would soon be open to me. I imagined all the wonders inside: books and maps and pictures of faraway places. Numbers written above or below each other, or side by side, that solved problems about how many apples or how much butter. Make-believe tales about fairies and princesses and little green elves. True stories about heroes and heroines and black-hearted pirates. History books telling about things that happened in the past to famous people. Poems to memorize. Experiments about how things worked. There would be thousands of things to arrange on the shelves of my mind. And new friends to talk to and play with. It all seemed too good to be true.

As I walked slowly home, I practiced my greeting to the teacher. "Good morning, Mister McLaughlin."

In the week that remained before school started, I continued to address the scarecrow as Mr. McLaughlin. I repeated nursery rhymes and sang songs to Irene. I read the first grade books to Howard and tried out all the sounds of the alphabet letters. While I practiced the tongue twisters, I finished the embroidery on my sampler. The open door was all stitched in white.

On the first day of school, I walked over with Ed, Caroline, and Frank, as I had done many times before. After the teacher came out and rang the bell, I stayed in the play yard and watched everyone else file into the building, as usual. Then I looked down to make sure my shoelaces were tied, smoothed my new blue calico dress, took a deep breath, and walked eagerly up the steps and through the open door.

"Good morning, Mister McLaughlin," I said. The words came out as clear as water from the well. "My name is Dora Cookson, and I'm going to be in your class this year."

I smiled until I could feel my dimples sink into deep holes. Oh, it is wonderful to know the good news and to be able to tell it!